Ex-Libris

The Burning Ground

Arriving at a French carpet factory near the Belgian border where he is to have discussions with the firm's technical expert as part of a proposed European merger, Tim Simpson of White's Bank finds the factory destroyed by fire and his prospective contact with it.

The factory was old, so its destruction and the death are suspicious, but the clues are both sparse and strange: a volume of Robert Graves's poetry; the site of his trench before the 1915 battle of Loos; a wartime painting by Nevinson in the Cubist-Futurist style.

The people involved are equally diverse: a brisk Belgian businessman; a Lancashire mill owner and his nephew; a powerful French entrepreneur; a blonde Marketing-mistress; a French ex-rugby player of Polish extraction; the Whites and the Maucourts, bankers of London and Paris, usually at loggerheads.

Caught in conflicts which are the legacy of terrible wars, Tim faces a tough assignment in locations ranging from Lancashire mills to the inside of French and Belgian police stations where he is held on a murder charge. The case needs all his penchant for art-biography, the help of his art-expert wife, Sue, his detective skill, and his rugby instincts.

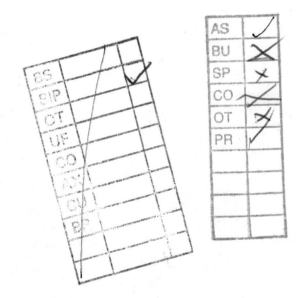

JOHN MALCOLM

The Burning Ground

A Tim Simpson mystery

THE CRIME CLUB
An Imprint of HarperCollins *Publishers*

First published in Great Britain in 1993
by The Crime Club, an imprint of
HarperCollins Publishers, 77–85 Fulham Palace Road,
Hammersmith, London W6 8JB

9 8 7 6 5 4 3 2 1

John Malcolm asserts the moral right to be identified
as the author of this work.

A catalogue record for this book is
available from the British Library

ISBN 0 00 232433 4

Photoset in Linotron Baskerville by
Rowland Phototypesetting Ltd
Bury St Edmunds, Suffolk
Printed and bound in Great Britain by
HarperCollins Book Manufacturing, Glasgow

0

The police inspector in charge of the case was called Claessens. He was a small, dark, fairly plump Belgian in a three-piece suit with a waistcoat that fitted much too tightly. Creases corrugated his buttoned stomach. On the whole he was grave but not unfriendly and his station's coffee was pretty good: strong but not bitter or overstewed. He and his sergeants listened to the story I told them several times before it was all written down and typed. Then I signed it. They went away and left me to be watched for quite a long time while nothing much seemed to happen.

If I were a smoker I'd have smoked a lot.

'It's always difficult,' the policeman watching me said gloomily, 'when it's an affair with French complications. Official channels, and all that. You wouldn't think, in 1992, that things were still so nationalistic.'

They took my Crombie away and gave me a receipt. They took swabs from my hands and carried off my shoes. After a while they gave me a hamburger and chips, with more coffee. That must have been about lunch-time. I fell asleep after eating it and was woken by Claessens returning with one of his sergeants, complete with notebook. They didn't start the tape-recorder in the interview room and I'm not sure what time it was.

'Your statement will be difficult to corroborate, Mr Simpson.'

That started to make me irritable. Unshaven, I am irritable anyway. With a sore neck I am much worse.

'But no doubt you will explain it all to the French police when they arrest you.'

'Eh?'

'When they arrest you. We will be taking you to the border to hand you over shortly. I can always get you back again if need be.'

'Shuttlecock and battledore,' I muttered.

'I beg your pardon?'

'Just an expression.'

Claessens stared at me for a while, then said, almost out of the blue, 'You have not explained why, when you were detained, you were looking in the bureau bookcase in the office. The security men were quite specific on that point. Your behaviour was odd.'

'Oh yes I have told you. I was looking for evidence. Disks, documents and so on.'

'Ah. Quite so. You did say that.' Claessens' eyes were on mine as he nodded. 'Surely you do not think, however, that anyone would place incriminating material in so obvious a spot?'

'You never can tell. There was a great detective who said that the obvious place is often the best.'

Claessens' Belgian expression became alert, defensive. 'Which great detective?'

'Oh, I don't know. Sherlock Holmes, probably.'

His expression relaxed and became slightly humorous. 'Ah. Possibly. I think it was Auguste Dupin, actually. Nevertheless, it seems unlikely that you would have found the material there.'

He stared at me again. You English, the stare said, you seem so ingenuous sometimes, but can you really be? What are you hiding from me?

I looked back at him as innocently as I could. He wouldn't have believed what I told him, anyway.

After another pause and a long stare. Claessens grunted. 'We will see. It is time to take you to France. I think we will be in contact again soon, Mr Simpson.'

'A pleasure, I'm sure.'

He grinned suddenly. 'You're a cool fellow. Very cool.'

'Thank you. I take that, from a Fleming, as a real compliment.'

We parted with some courtesy. They took me in a van, all of forty minutes or so, to Tourcoing, and in no time I was in a French police station, with a French police inspector and sergeant sitting in front of me, filling in forms. I made the same set of statements, had my fingerprints taken, saw my Crombie overcoat being carried around in a transparent plastic bag like a dry cleaner's, had a small black coffee, ate a sandwich.

Much later on they brought me a hamburger and chips. The gastronomic border was imperceptible.

I had plenty of time to rub my face with my hands, scratch my head, and think back extensively over the events which had brought me to this closely-guarded condition.

Thus it must be with a life of crime.

1

It was starting to rain as the sign for Auchy-les-Mines came up on my left and I stopped the rental car right there, on the N41 between La Bassée and Cambrin. Thin drops speckled the windscreen like spray from a distant sea. My route map indicated that Cuinchy and Givenchy would now be to my right and some instinct told me that I must be parked in what must have been No-Man's-Land, half way between the two lines of trenches which once crossed the main road.

It was an unexceptional scene typical of Northern France, with tiled and plastered houses dotted to my left, where the outskirts of Auchy clustered loosely up to the edge of the road, and more open country to the north, beyond the canal. In the distance the spire of Béthune would soon be spiking a lowering sky; to the south lay Vermelles, Loos, Lens and slagheaps.

Dark clouds scudded over the sad landscape, still celebrated for sudden death and punctuated by cemeteries.

I turned right, off the main road, and drove over a high, narrow bridge, noting that the canal widened here to what must have been the equivalent of a watery siding, where barges once passed or loaded at stone-edged quays. The terrible brickstacks had probably stood to my left, along the canal to Cuinchy, but there was no sign of them now. The local road became small and twisty, studded with the clean little graveyards fronted by obelisks that the War Graves Commission maintains, but the land was open, flattening out beyond the canal and old mine workings. My visibility was shortening, although here and there you could see that new houses had been built on isolated plots, as though wanting to brick over bits of the awful local history.

Fat chance they stood of doing that.

North of Cuinchy, circling round towards Givenchy and Festubert, I came across two saloon cars parked beside the road, one a left-hand drive Jaguar with a Dordogne registration, the other a Renault 25 with Belgian plates. I parked carefully behind the Renault and got out into a freshening, showery wind, noting the green fields sprouting winter cereal shoots and villages across the hedges, not so far away.

Three men stood huddled on the verge looking at me expectantly, one surreptitiously checking his watch. This was the tall, spare figure of Sir Richard White; the other two were new to me.

'Tim! Well done! You must have moved fast.' Sir Richard held his hand out and I took it for a dry, firm shake. 'It was kind of you to get here so promptly.'

It was a gracious courtesy because kindness did not come into this excursion. I was responding to an order.

'Hello, Richard,' I said respectfully. 'Your directions were as impeccable as ever.'

He smiled slightly and I noted his glance run up and down me with approval. Sir Richard White, of White's Bank, is a thin, spare figure, rather grey in hair and drawn in looks but still an active seventy-year-old, who divides his time equally between England and France, where he has a house in the Dordogne and the use of a flat in Paris. He turned to the other two men to make introductions.

'Tim, you haven't met Bob Janssens. Bob has kindly come over from Courtrai to show us the way.'

I stretched forward to shake. Janssens was a steel-spectacled Belgian in a steel-grey suit and fawn Burberry, fortyish, but his smile was warm and he pumped my hand briskly.

'Mr Simpson. This is a pleasure. Sir Richard has told me

much about you. I am glad that we may be going to work together and that you could make it today. It is a good start, I think.'

I made an affirmative reply. Janssens was fitter than I'd imagined, not conforming to the chip-eating Belgian physique beloved of Dutch caricature—the Dutch tell Belgian jokes as we tell Irish ones—and under the well-tailored clothes the frame was strong. His face was sunburnt and his blue eyes were set in clear whites. I put him down as a swimmer, a frequenter of beaches or pools, but not an idler.

I was already turning to meet the other man.

'Tim, this is Jack Ashworth. Jack, this is Tim Simpson.'

The contrast with the Belgian couldn't have been more exaggerated. Ashworth was huge. A great stomach swelled under his battered blue raincoat, open to reveal the strained pinstripes of a vast, baggy, traditional British business suit. His dark clothes flapped in the rain-gusting breeze like ruffled feathers on a flustered rook. Craggy features as battered as the mackintosh were set to the front of a big head jammed on a fat neck strangled by a soft white shirt collar, from which sprouted a kipper tie disfigured by a wince-inducing Paisley design.

He folded my hand into a huge, sausage-fingered grip and did his best to crush the bones.

'How do?' he said grandly, his Lancashire accent parting the wind. 'How are you goin'? All right?'

Somewhere like Bury, I thought; north of Manchester anyway, where the accent gets a curl to it that you can't mistake. A textile trade man, down to the toecaps of his vast brown brogues.

'Fine,' I said, retrieving the hand undamaged. 'I'm fine, thanks.'

'Aye,' he said, casting an eye about him, 'you look in good fettle. Can't say as there's much by way of mill chimneys here, though.'

He grinned, looking back at me slyly, as though sharing a mischievous joke. Janssens was quick to respond.

'Indeed not, Mr Ashworth. Not here. Our meeting with Pierre Martens at Wingles has been fixed for ten this morning and since we are so near I thought that Sir Richard would enjoy a little diversion, just five minutes, on our way.'

'Oh, aye?'

'Yes. You see I happen to know that Sir Richard is very interested in battlefields. Historic battlefields. Isn't that correct, Sir Richard?'

The spare grey figure inclined its head gracefully. Janssens was right. I wondered, though, whether he realized that Sir Richard's interest was in the sites of the Hundred Years' War, in the knightly armour and arrows deployed at Crécy, Agincourt and the Dordogne, not the howitzers and trenches of 1914. Still, Janssens was obviously anxious to humour the old buzzard; it wouldn't have done to interrupt him as he raised his voice to beat the spattery breeze.

'We are very near the site of the battle of Loos. In 1915, your poet Robert Graves was here and described the scene very accurately.' Janssens smiled modestly. 'I have always admired his work—the TV version of *I, Claudius*, for instance, which we much enjoyed in Belgium—and I recently had the pleasure of going to Deya, in Mallorca, where he lived for so many years.'

So that was where the tan came from. Holidays in Mallorca, with a bit of Graves-grafting thrown in. An unusual Belgian, this.

Janssens had turned to point across the field beside us. His voice took on the ring of the guided-tour courier, lifting again to make itself heard.

'Over there, Auchy, with Haisnes behind. Half-right there was a pithead and slag heaps, now gone. Half-left to La Bassée, where the sun caught the weather-vane, making it glint so that Graves could see, quite clearly, the German sector. He observed through a periscope, of course, from somewhere in the middle of this field, where his head-quarters trench was sited. He described it as a flat meadow full of cornflowers, with marguerites and poppies in the long grass by the barbed wire. There was a wreck of an aeroplane in it and he saw a big house, ruined by shelling, about three-quarters of a mile off. La Bassée was on the German side; they shouted across the trenches to the Tommies that the French girls there were most obliging—*très bien pour coucher avec.*'

Janssens grinned wittily and paused, as though self-conscious of his own enthusiasm, then looked at Sir Richard for approval. The old banker's face was quite a picture.

'Remarkable,' he said, with genuine feeling, as he gazed across the now-peaceful fields towards the spire of La Bassée. 'Quite remarkable. You must have an extraordinary memory, Bob. Where on earth did you find out all this?'

Janssens smiled his delight. 'Thank you. Since boyhood I have always read everything of Graves I could find—what an extraordinary man he was—and all this can be read in his famous book, *Goodbye To All That*, you see.'

Sir Richard nodded, sagely. 'Ah. Of course. A milestone of a book.' His gaze flicked to me. 'Have you read it, Tim? Not your generation, perhaps, but—'

'I've read it,' I said.

'Jack?'

''Appen as not. Can't say as I 'ave. Poetry, is it?'

Sir Richard smiled and put back his head.

> *'It was not foes to conquer,*
> *Nor sweethearts to be kind,*
> *But it was friends to die for*
> *That I would seek and find.'*

His voice carried the verse perfectly, with no difficulty in breathing. Janssens stared at him enraptured. The Hundred Years' War was obviously only the iceberg-tip of Sir Richard's many cultural interests. Ashworth goggled a rather blood-pressured goggle from above his throttled collar and cast a querying eye upon me, but I kept my face straight; the verse is A. E. Housman, of course, not Graves, although the sentiment was dead accurate.

'Graves *was* remarkable. I do agree with you, Bob. Remarkable family.' Sir Richard adopted a reminiscent tone. 'Father of Anglo-Irish stock descended from a French knight of the Norman Conquest. *Graves*—' he altered the pronunciation to that of the French Bordeaux wine—'d'you prefer the white or the red, Tim?'

'Both,' I said promptly, and Ashworth grinned at me.

'Mother,' Sir Richard went on, unperturbed, 'Amy von Ranke. German. Well, Saxon to be pedantic. Graves had a favourite cousin fighting on the other side. We forget how small Europe is.'

Janssens nodded enthusiastically. 'This is true. So very true. We Europeans are much closer than we think. The Englishman Robert Graves was of French, Irish, and German stock yet fought in the Royal Welch Fusiliers. A great writer. I had not realized, Sir Richard, that you knew his work so intimately.'

'No.' Sir Richard had gone a bit dry. 'Well. You weren't to, were you? But your instincts were excellent. This has been a most fortuitous diversion, Bob. Almost inspired. I'm very grateful to you. Good heavens! So this is where Graves actually was when Loos was fought. Not an auspicious occasion. He was quite bitter about it, I seem to recall.'

His gaze had gone back out across the fields and I could imagine the images of trench warfare he was mentally conceiving: mud, wire, shellholes and horrid rotting bodies among iron wrecks. Stumps and ruins; before his time as well as before mine, but vivid in the nation's memory still. Terror and hideous death: as with the field of the battle of Waterloo, it seemed on a much smaller scale than I'd imagined, like scenes of childhood revisited.

Ashworth almost physically shook himself as another cold sprinkle of rain spotted his ruffled bulk.

'Right,' he said, with an air of finality, gesturing out- wards. 'That's quite something, that is. I mean, to find the place so accurately after all these years.' He turned to me as he stepped back heavily from the verge. 'Ain't it?'

I nearly chuckled out loud. He could not have conveyed a desire to be off more graphically if he'd tried. The poet Robert Graves and the images of this field did not appeal to his imagination in the slightest. Rain was coming and business awaited, that was what his expression conveyed. Business was what he wanted to be at, not this fartarsing about with fairy poets and filled-in trenches.

'Remarkable,' I said neutrally, to agree with him, then looked at my watch. It was past ten o'clock. 'I think that Bob Janssens has given us all a fascinating detour. As Eng- lishmen I'm sure we all much appreciate it. Perhaps, how- ever, we should now—'

'Get on our way,' Sir Richard agreed, his pale eyes light- ing humorously on me. 'I'm sure we are all anxious to talk to Mr Martens. Bob?'

'Of course.' Janssens smiled cheerfully. He seemed to be pleased with his little history excursion and had not noticed any anxiety to be off. He looked at his watch as though to confirm my timekeeping. 'It is most certainly time. I am so pleased to have been here and to have been able to show it to you. We will go to Wingles now. It's just a few minutes. Will you follow me?'

He set off towards the Renault and Sir Richard, eyeing his own Jaguar, looked dubiously at my rental car. Ash-

worth settled any debate on passengers with a finality that
brooked no argument.

'I'll go with Tim here,' he said flatly. 'Want a word in
his shell-like.'

Sir Richard inclined gracefully. Janssens was getting into
his Renault. Ashworth and I clambered into the rental job,
which lurched dangerously to his side as he dumped himself
heavily into the passenger seat.

'Wrong side, any road,' he grumbled. 'Hard to get used
to.'

Janssens went off first, followed by Sir Richard's Jaguar.
I navigated the twisty, open lanes a short distance behind.
Ashworth appeared to forget the trench-history immedi-
ately.

'Sir Richard tells me you're a rugby man,' he grunted,
fumbling at his safety-belt with his huge sausage fingers.

'That's right. Well, I was. Haven't played for a long
time.'

'Union?'

'Yes.'

'I'm for the League, meself,' he said, baring his teeth in
a grin. 'Allus was.'

'Wigan or St Helens?'

'Neither. Warrington.'

I raised my eyebrows. Warrington is a bit to the west
and south, I thought, for a man of your accent. What's
more, it's in Cheshire. Janssens was slowing down as we
got back to the Cambrin–La Bassée road and appeared to
be going straight across into Auchy-les-Mines. He waited
cautiously for us to catch up before crossing.

'Me uncle in Warrington took me in as a boy. Did me
apprenticeship in the mill there. I'm from Rawtenstall,
really.' It was as though Ashworth had read my mind. 'I've
always preferred League, any road.'

He shot me a glance and I grinned. 'It's a good game.

But where it used to be Oglethorpe passing it to Rams-bottom and Satterthwaite punting an up-and-under, it's all Edwards and Williams and Jones, now.'

He chuckled. 'You're dead right there. Welshmen all over. It's the money, ain't it?'

'It is.'

'Your lot'll be going for the brass soon, mark my words. Won't they?'

'I'm afraid they will.'

His deep-set, almost piggy eyes narrowed in his bloated, craggy face. 'Cambridge, were you? That's what Sir Richard said.'

'Yes, I was.'

'You'd be all for the amateur, then. It won't do, you know. Not with that brass coming from the gate. The players have got to get on with it, now.'

'I agree. I'm afraid you're right. But it won't be the same game.'

We were following Janssens south through Auchy-les-Mines with its brick church spire, seen by Graves through his trench periscope, and a sign to Vermelles to the right. Vermelles was taken and re-taken eight times in one month of 1915; somewhere between here and Cambrin was a big farmhouse called Les Briques, where the old woman who looked after Graves at Annezin had had a fling during the Franco-Prussian war of 1870 with a *petit-caporal* who made her pregnant. She lost the child and here, forty-four years later, death had returned to splinter the streets. Les Briques; bricks were very prevalent hereabouts and Graves's crowd had had to fight in and out of the unpredict-able stacks, hand to hand sometimes, in a horrible contest with only one statistical outcome, sure as fate.

I've read *Goodbye To All That*.

Everyone else should, too.

We crossed the D947 at Haisnes, then passed through

Douvrin, entering a maze of small roads to the south, where old industries that had overspilled from Lens filled narrow roads with mean terraced houses and factories that were coated with thick foundry dust. Drizzle blew sharply between gaps, rocking the rental car. Ashworth looked about him with satisfaction.

'Its just like Radcliffe used to be,' he said, cheering up. 'Or back streets of Bacup.'

I grinned. The outskirts of Lille are not unlike the north-west of England, with the same rusty industries—textiles, coal, engineering—struggling to keep their chimneys smoking. The weather's no better, either.

'You'll be a dab hand at the carpet trade, then?' Ashworth, feeling more at home, was moving to the attack. Merchant bankers like me would be fair game for sarcasm.

'I know my needlefelts from my Wiltons,' I said, humping the car over a narrow railway bridge that shot even Ashworth's bulk, strapped to its seat, upwards for his head to collide with the roof. Janssens had veered into a side lane that followed sagging cables and long wide sheds with generous eaves, like stretched Swiss chalets dipped in brick dust and cinders, to an end across railway lines and loading bays. The front of a new building, architected in high-tech red girders squared round brick facings, stuck out beyond the old engine sheds of a disused siding.

And ended there.

As we pulled up, a pungent smell of charred fabric and burnt chemicals penetrated the rental car's ventilation system. In front of us two fire engines stood in puddled cinders, coils of hose disappearing towards the back of the building.

Except that there was no back of the building. The red-girdered façade was all that remained. Behind it great clouds of black smoke, shot through by terrifying bursts of flame, billowed towards a watery sky historically no stranger to explosions.

'Bugger me,' Ashworth said, struggling to release his seat-belt with his tight fat fingers. 'Bloody heck.'

A great heap of smouldering, charred rubbish was piled beneath twisted stanchions and distorted trusses. A wall had collapsed to reveal blackened machinery filled with charcoaled, bubbling gunge of some sort, blistering in heat. A caped gendarme stood in front of Janssens' car, preventing him going any further. We found ourselves in a group, cars abandoned, remonstrating with him in the rain whilst flinching from the sight before us.

'*Impossible!*' He blocked Janssens' path with unmistakable solidity.

'Monsieur Martens!' Janssens was shouting. 'Where in hell is Monsieur Martens? The manager?'

The gendarme was joined by a sergeant of impressive bulk, who more than doubled the barrier to us. Janssens began to argue vehemently and looked as if he'd have to be restrained. A mushroom-ball of orange fire parted the smoke above the factory roof, billowing so broadly that its heat made us cringe in ignorance of the dirty drizzle falling on our group. A knot of firemen appeared round a corner, hauling on a stiff hose. From behind the sergeant appeared an old man in *bleu de travail* who Janssens leapt at with a cry.

'Dubois! The caretaker! *Où est-il?* Where is he? Where is Pierre Martens? What's happened?'

The old man blinked and made a gesture at the crackling framework behind him. '*Il est là, Monsieur Janssens.*'

'*Là?* There? Where?'

The French are nothing if not practical and the old man's gesture was unmistakable.

'*Carbonisé,*' he said, darkly.

'*Carbonisé?*' Janssens' voice filled with horror.

'*Oui, monsieur.*' The old man nodded emphatically. 'Mr Martens is somewhere in there. It's a furnace. Terrible. There'll be practically nothing left. Parts of poor Martens must be coating the girders by now, down past the yarn store somewhere.'

2

'It is really quite bewildering.' Jeremy White gazed at me ruminatively from behind his Georgian mahogany partners' desk. 'You take on these European responsibilities, you move, as it were, into the realms of Uncle Richard's high falutin' trans-national investment projects, you part company with us mundane, everyday London workers—mere hewers of wood and drawers of water—and yet, quite characteristically, you come sailing into my office with a *Wunderkind*'s bland smile and announce that you have perpetrated yet another massive disaster. I am, as I say, bewildered. I thought that such things were of the past.'

'Jeremy—'

'I ask myself, and I ask myself seriously now, can the leopard change its spots? The elephant shed its trunk? The smile on the face lose its tiger?'

'Jeremy, do not enjoy yourself unduly over this matter. The unpleasant death of Mr Martens is not an item for unseemly badinage.'

'Badinage! Ha! Is that what you call it now? Badinage? Not banter any more? We have become so francophone, have we?'

'What is more, the proposed, potentially lucrative investment the bank has sponsored in putting together the Dillworth Carpet Company of Lancashire, Tapis Rossignol of France and Louis Janssens of Belgium is threatened by what looks like a very nasty fire. A very nasty fire indeed.'

A look of smug satisfaction spread over Jeremy's face. 'Marry in haste, repent at leisure,' he murmured.

'There's no need to gloat. Just because you didn't like

the deal in the first place it is not pleasant to enjoy this disaster. It was a horrible thing; you didn't see it.'

'Disaster?' He raised his eyebrows. 'Disaster? Surely the company was insured? Fully insured for loss of both assets and operating profits?'

I hesitated as I ignored his deliberate omission of the late Pierre Martens from his definition of a disaster. Finance before flesh, as with so many City matters, it seemed. 'I believe so, yes.'

'Believe? Believe? Do you not know? Have you not ascertained?'

I gave him a nettled look. It was all very well for him. He was sitting comfortably in his office at White's Bank in Gracechurch Street. He had not been called over at a moment's notice to join the meeting Sir Richard had arranged between the principals from England and Belgium with a key manager in France. He had simply sat there and predicted it would all end in tears. As with Thatcher for Europe, so Jeremy White for the big carpet deal, the BCD, as it had come to be known at the Bank.

'I have,' I said defensively, 'been assigned to this affair for precisely forty-eight hours now. Twenty-four of them have been spent motoring the tomb-laden lanes around Lille and gaping at the lethal result of one of the worst factory fires I've ever seen. Quite apart from dealing with a distinctly shaken Sir Richard and a music-hall version of a Lancashire mill-owner called Ashworth, who needed six pints of strong lager to get his nerves back together while complaining loudly that it wasn't Tetley's bitter, or some such northern brew.'

Jeremy grinned. Jeremy was enjoying himself. He had reluctantly accepted his uncle's prior claim on my services as an inevitable result of restructuring at the Bank, which was having to adjust to newer, harder, times. He did not like the idea that I now had a European role which took

precedence over his interests and was determined by Sir
Richard, but he had to acquiesce. The call to present myself
at Wingles had come from Sir Richard's Paris office, where
he kept half his time at Maucourt Frères, the new partner
of White's Bank in France. I had been following the BCD
affair with interest but only half an eye, since Sir Richard
and Eugène Maucourt, aided and abetted by a minor bevy
of investment specialists, were the prime movers in this
ambitious but not particularly unusual project. All of a
sudden my presence had been requested; Sir Richard was
in need of support.

'He should have known,' Jeremy gloated, 'from past
experience, that you only have to breathe on a project for
mayhem to ensue. I, of course, have sustained the nervous
strain of your licentious involvements unaided for years. It
comes, I must say, as a relief to have someone else to share
the burden, although Uncle Richard may not quite see his
role in that light.'

I stared at him sadly. 'All this,' I murmured, 'this
depreciation and obloquy, simply because a factory caught
fire.'

'Ha! Simply! Where you are concerned nothing can be
simple. The only blessing, from my point of view, is that
for once the Art Fund is not involved and therefore no
further load will fall upon my aching shoulders.'

This was unfair. The Art Fund of White's Bank, an
investment arrangement for clients wishing to have a flutter
on the art market, was something Jeremy and I had started
some years back. It had done well, even if the pursuit of
certain artefacts and canvases had occasioned criminal
involvements. Jeremy had been just as much a prime mover
as I, who had to do the groundwork and the running. The
fact that I had to deal with the practical manifestations of
greed, forgery and felonies of various sorts rising to murder
while he, typically, kept safely in his office, was not some-

thing for him to twist into claims for sympathy and credit. Jeremy loved the Art Fund and was as responsible for what had happened as much as anyone.

'Ah,' I said carefully, poised for my moment at last. 'Talking of shoulders, Sir Richard rather felt that yours might be able to help. With the burdens you mention so freely.'

'Eh?' His expression of smug satisfaction vanished in a flash.

'To help. In fact, he rather felt that you might *like* to help.'

'Me?' Panic appeared in his features. 'Me? Wha—why? What with?'

'Your long-standing friendship with the Ashworth family. You were at Oxford with Jack's nephew Philip, weren't you?'

A scowl darkened his eyebrows. 'Philip? Me?'

'Yes. Philip. You. I looked up the old files, the extremely old files, and I found that you actually introduced the Dillworth Carpet Company to us as a client. It was from your friendship with Philip Ashworth at College. You sailed together in some sort of dinghy races, didn't you?'

'Good God! That was ages ago!'

'Of course. And I must say you have kept remarkably quiet about it. Very quiet about it indeed.'

'Well, why shouldn't I?' he spluttered. 'Great Scott, a hell of a lot of water has gone under numerous bridges since I steered the Ashworths in our direction. It was never treated as an account of mine. Just an introduction. The Ashworths never used us that much. Canny, cunning lot of Lancashire weavers, or whatever. Held on to their brass with grim determination.'

'We helped finance several expansions and you know it. Not to mention their takeover of two smaller companies.'

'We may well have. And I may have been aware of it.

But, as you know only too well, my years at Park Lane and in the insurance bond market resulted in my exclusion from much of the Bank's affairs. I was kept back even from my own contacts. You and I, my dear Tim, are still relative newcomers to the Bank's core business in this country. As for Europe—' he made a dismissive gesture—'I have never been closely consulted on affairs over there.'

It was a wonderful misrepresentation, compounded of half-truths carefully selected from the events of recent years. Park Lane had been Jeremy's very own personal finance business, and it was true that the Bank had kept him, as a junior member of a cadet branch of the family, at arm's length for years. The relationship between himself and his uncle, Sir Richard, then chairman, had always been difficult. But Jeremy had voted enthusiastically for our liaison with Maucourt Frères and his relationship with other overseas branches was close. Insularity was not one of Jeremy's characteristics.

'None the less,' I continued remorselessly, 'Sir Richard felt that the deployment of your undoubted talents and personal relationships might assist in what has become a more difficult phase of the project. The Bank's role, and hence the Bank's potential fees, must be safeguarded.'

'A more difficult phase! My God! You're talking like Jacques Delors himself! The key manager in the French organization is conveniently fried to a crisp, leaving some excellent questions unanswered, and you refer to the event as a "more difficult phase". This is Common Marketspeak at its most obscurantist.'

My eyes narrowed. 'Key manager? Excellent questions? Jeremy, you have been following this affair much closer than you should. Haven't you?'

He flinched. 'What do you mean, should? Should? I am a director of this Bank. It is my solemn duty to follow such matters. A duty laid down by law.'

'You cunning, underhand old devil. Out of all the multifarious things that are going on, you pick on this. You absolute conniver. You've been watching everything all along, haven't you?'

'Indeed I have not!'

His denial rang just a tone off-key. Too defensive. I gave him a penetrating stare and he met my eye with not quite just enough confidence.

'Jeremy, I have to go up to the Dillworth Carpet Company tomorrow to see Jack Ashworth and get myself briefed. Will you come with me?'

'Certainly not! I have many other commitments!'

'Such as?'

'That's my business! How dare you!'

'Jeremy, Sir Richard thinks that, in the circumstances, it would be a good idea for you to come to Dillworth's and renew your friendship with your old chum Philip. If it needs renewing. There is much knowledge we must glean.'

'I shall do no such thing! I wouldn't dream of imposing myself on an old acquaintance for commercial gain. Anyway, I am a director of the Bank and have much better things to occupy myself with than scouting about as a squeaker beneath a bank of carpet looms!'

'Thank you, Jeremy. Your definition of my role is so attractive. And commercial gain is what we are here for, so I do think that it would be a good idea if you came.'

'Oh you do, do you? You would. Well, I shan't. I see nothing to be gained by my presence in this ill-considered affair. None whatever.'

He didn't actually pout or throw his rattle out of his pram but the tone was quite unmistakable. There's no dealing with Jeremy once you've worked him into one of these moods. I rose to go.

'Sir Richard,' I said, as my parting shot, 'may take a very different view.'

He gave me a crushing stare. I have to admit it was a
pretty weak closing line, but then who was I but a minion,
caught between him and Sir Richard?

Try the Gospel according to St Matthew, Chapter 6,
verse 24, for a line on that situation.

3

North from Bolton the road rises over the bare shoulders of mist-shrouded uplands that lead to Turton Moor. Long stone walls, disappearing straight over summits, contain the stubby, peaty grass that random, grimy sheep stoop to graze. Behind you the remaining chimneystacks of Bolton appear in the rear-view mirror like a diluted L. S. Lowry in miniature. Soon the miserable upland rawness is ruined by plantations of Christmas-tree conifers above the reservoir. To your left the exposed valley sweeps downward under the long ridge towards Winter Hill, and beyond that, Rivington Pike. From the congestion of Bolton and the northern edges of the straggling city of Manchester you emerge into emptiness, low skies and bleak moors punctuated by wet, dark stone buildings sited at inexplicable intervals. You are on your way over Turton, as they say locally, pronouncing it —over Turton—as though you were crossing the Andes.

Rolling down the streaming road the other side, as the sign for Hoddlesdon comes up on your right, you face the small stone town of Darwen, crouched under its famous chimneystack that is said to be modelled on the more celebrated campanile of Venice. A Venetian might not appreciate the comparison but, in its massive square solemnity and sooty top-heaviness, it is at least a change from the multitude of its round-sectioned brick companions. Ahead lies Blackburn and beyond that the open fells of the Forest of Bowland, guarding the way to the Lake District and the empty reaches up to Carlisle. It's no wonder the locals have a feeling of being near the outer edge of populated England. Europe might just as well be in China.

'Ee,' Jack Ashworth said, dropping into the vernacular

as his secretary guided me into his office, 'tha's bloody early, I'll say that for tha'. Where've you come from? Did you stay at the Last Drop overnight or summat?'

I shook my head. 'First shuttle up to Manchester,' I said briskly. The drive over the cold moors had woken me up.

'The 6.45? By God, you're keen. It must have been on time into Ringway too.' He looked at his watch. 'You've not half made shift. It's not nine yet. What'll you have? Tea or coffee?'

'Tea, thanks.'

His secretary smiled a comfortable, middle-aged smile as Ashworth waved an empty cup from his desk at her.

'I'll get another pot for you, Mr Jack,' she said.

'And some of those nice biscuits, Doris love. Mr Simpson here'll be fair clemmed. Sit you down, Tim. Get your breath back. I must say I'm still shell-shocked from me visit to France.'

He gave me a sly look. He didn't look a bit shell-shocked. He wasn't wearing the disgraceful tie and the baggy suit, either. A crisp white collar of more than adequate diameter circled his huge neck and his admirably-ironed shirt front gleamed behind a dark, spotted silk tie. A charcoal grey suit of excellent cut made him look half the size. His features were still craggy and swollen, but not nearly as gross as they had seemed. Ho, I thought, so that's the game: here in his headquarters he's the respected head of the clan, the senior Mr Jack, someone to be proud of: out there he's the badly-dressed, parochial Lancastrian hamming it up to make sure the opposition contemptuously drops its guard. This is one to watch very carefully. I sat down and took a quick look around.

Over the mantelpiece of his solid, warm, sash-windowed office was an original landscape by Lowry, not as good as the one that used to be in the entrance hall of the Tate but not a minor one, either. The whites of the background were

fresh and crisp, emphasizing the reds of the mill buildings,
the black chimneys, the strange, capering, knob-legged
people. I supposed a Lowry was almost *de rigueur* for a
Manchester art-lover but my eye caught, on a further wall,
a small Cubist painting of stylized marching men and I
whistled, softly.

'What's up?' The Lancastrian accent wasn't nearly as
pronounced.

'That's a Nevinson,' I said. 'As good as any, including
the Tate's. From his best period.'

He didn't say anything. Across his face there came a look,
something spurred by an emotion, deep and indefinable. I
got up, mainly to avoid looking at him, for I felt I had
intruded, and yet the painting was there in his office, in
public.

'Around 1916,' I said, looking closer. 'Smaller than the
famous *Column on the March*, but of the same type. Superb,
and very rare.'

I looked at it for a moment longer, taking in the burning
sky and the thorny bristle of men and guns marching over
interminable wet cobbles and mud to their inevitable fate.
Never was Cubism more graphically employed; all that
bombast and pre-war rhetoric concentrated, after Nevinson's experience, to create vivid images of doomed soldiers
like helpless tin toys on their way to be smashed. The little
painting arrested me as much as had Bob Janssens' diversion. Not to mention its horrific aftermath.

A compelling comparison.

At that moment Ashworth's secretary came in with a
tray of tea and biscuits, a big brown pot weighing the metal
tray heavily to one side, so that I sprang to help her. The
interruption broke whatever it was that had made him go
into a reverie. He waited for the secretary to pour out
ceremoniously and leave, then looked at me over a large
white pottery cup of steaming tea.

'I've been checking on you,' he said. He was a big man, even in the charcoal suit, and his presence bulked behind the cup, dwarfing it.

'Oh, really?' The tea was excellent; they have such wonderful water in that area, soft and springy, ideal for washing cotton.

'Yes, really. Mate o' mine in the League game has pals at Sale. You know? Sale Rugby Club?'

'Know it well,' I said, accepting a thick shortbread biscuit from a thick pottery plate redolent of steam railway provenance. 'Even played there, in my day.'

'Aye. Well my pal asked his pal—the League does talk to the Union—and he said that you were quite a goer. They knew you, at Sale, they did.' He squiggled his eyebrows at me. 'Front row, they said.'

'Oh? Well. I'm sure they did. I was, too.'

'You don't look like a front row man to me.'

'Well, there you are. That's the amateur game for you. I'm probably not quite the build.'

'Front row men, to me, are bloody great thick thugs with heads to match.'

I bit on the biscuit, scattering flaky crumbs on my suit. 'Not far wrong, I'd say.'

He grinned. 'They said that you were as good a goer off the field as on. After the match, they meant.'

'I was younger then. Intemperate. You know how youth is.'

His face changed to express concern. 'Ee, never say die, lad. I can give most of my young fellers two pints start and see 'em under t'table, Saturday night.'

I eyed him carefully. I wasn't surprised. Bulk like his can absorb heroic quantities of ale. With practice.

'You didn't do too badly in France,' he said, almost accusingly. 'I noticed. I were right shaken so I downed my pints a bit hasty like, but you kept up.'

'It was probably the shock to me, too.'

'We'll come to that in a minute. The thing is, this contact of mine, he said that you were, or rather are, the bright spark behind White's Art Fund. That's what he said.'

'Ah. Well. That was kind of him. I do manage the Fund, yes.'

'Thought so. Have you got a Lowry in your Fund?'

My eyes went automatically to the one over his mantelpiece. 'No, we haven't.'

'Why not? Why haven't you got a Lowry? You specialize in British art, don't you?'

'Never found one good enough. His best was marvellous, like the one at the Tate, but there's an awful lot I'd leave behind.'

His eyes narrowed. He jerked his head towards the mantelpiece. 'Is that one good enough?'

'Almost. Not quite. No offence, it's a valuable painting, but it's not for the Fund.'

He smiled slightly. 'I suspect you're not as impressed by Lowry as we are up here, but I like an honest answer. Don't worry, I'm not trying to sell it. The thing that interests me is you looked at that but you didn't get up for it. It was the Nevinson as had you on your pins.'

'Yes. It's much rarer. And it's great.'

He nodded slowly, got up, put down his big pottery cup and went over to stand in front of the Nevinson. 'I only hung that up a couple of days ago. It's supposed to be unlucky for our family but I said to Doris, since I'm off to France I'll stick that up, say nowt, and see what happens. I'm not superstitious and it's too good to hide away. Then when Janssens took us to that place it gave me a shiver, I can tell you. My brother were dead keen on Graves's poetry —always carried a thin book of it with him—and he's dead too, killed in the second lot. Painting weren't up in anyone's house then, as far as I know. But bugger me, you went straight to it.'

'It's unmistakable.'

He didn't listen. 'My grandfather bought that painting,' he said, staring at it. 'He bought it straight out of the Leicester Galleries in London in 1916. I've got the invoice. It were a fantastic exhibition. The best piece was called *La Patrie*. Arnold Bennett bought that. You know? Arnold Bennett of *Clayhanger*? My grandfather said as how they were the best paintings of the war as he'd ever seen, and he would've known—he was in the East Lancashires, you see. That painting's been at home in the family since then.'

'You must keep it.'

He looked at me sharply. 'Why d'you say that?'

'You must keep it because it's obviously important to you and your family. And you don't need the money. Even if you did want to sell it, now's not the time, not while the market's down. That would be my advice.'

'You mean your Fund wouldn't want it?'

'My Fund would buy it like a shot. We'd buy any important British painting that was available as long as the price was right and we had the cash in hand.'

'Well then, if you bought it now you'd get a bargain, wouldn't you?' His northern aggression wasn't hostile; just the normal test of mettle. They don't go for soft conversation much.

'I'm not here to take advantage of a client. You must hang on to that.'

My voice must have gone a bit sharp as the mood moved into the imperative. His eyes twinkled in his craggy face. 'Don't you even want first refusal?'

'Oh, that I'll have, certainly. But I'd be sad to take it off you.'

He nodded slowly, the twinkle fading. 'I'd be sad, too. My grandfather bought that on leave. He were killed

shortly after. On the Somme. They said my great-grand-
father were never the same after that. Wouldn't have this
painting up in the house. Everyone said it were bad luck.
It's always been hidden away, like.'

He looked at the painting again ruminatively and I felt
the same sense of intrusion as I stared at him, something
shaping in my mind, something I couldn't quite put my
finger on but existing, forming itself, as I phrased my response to him.

'It was Nevinson's misfortune that his greatest work
showed something everyone wanted to forget.'

He nodded slowly, glanced at me, came round the desk
and sat down. 'I've never met anyone before who knew
anything much about him. Nevinson, I mean. You seem to
have made quite a study of him.'

'No, not really. It's just that, well, there are parallels
with other artists. Nevinson went on painting until he died
in 1946. But there were only a few paintings to rival that
1916 exhibition. Futurism and Cubism combined to make
the most powerful images of the war. I'll dig some stuff up
for you if you like and photocopy it. Send it to you.'

'Thanks. Thanks a lot.' He picked up the pot. 'Another?'

'Please.'

'We must get on.'

'I suppose so.'

'Gassing about art.' He grinned. 'My lot wouldn't believe
it. Not of me. I'm glad you approve of that, though. I meant
what I said; first refusal's yours. If ever.' He almost shook
himself, the way he had at Cuinchy. You could tell that the
subject was closed to him; he cleared his craggy features as
he got back to business. 'Where do you want to start?'

I put down my pottery cup. 'We'd better leave the fire
out of it just for the moment, while I get my bearings. It's
going to be several days before the assessors make a report,

quite apart from the *pompiers*, who were not impressed. The heat was terrible. Christ, that was a fire.'

He produced a grim smile. 'Carpet backings aren't all jute these days, Tim. There's still a lot of latex about for secondary backings, quite apart from bitumen for carpet tiles. Flammability standards have affected all of us but the basic materials have to be brought in before they're processed. That lot had some polyurethane foam backings as well. If you've ever seen untreated polyurethane foam set on fire you'll not have forgotten it—it's the next thing to a fireball, an explosion. Terrible.'

'Surely there have to be safeguards for all these things?'

''Course there are. That's why the fire chiefs and the insurance men will want to ask some very hard questions. Shook me, it did. Damn lucky no one else was killed.'

His eye caught mine significantly. I thought of Jeremy, and the late Mr Martens, but decided to take this step by step.

'When the report comes, then we'll all have something to discuss. But for the moment I'm a new boy and I wanted to find out a bit about technical development.'

His smile was still grim. 'Now that's an interesting place to start. I wonder why you've chosen that?'

'It's one of the key areas. Now that woven carpets like Axminster and Wiltons are a small section of the market, you've abandoned your speed shuttle work and concentrated on the tufted carpet sector. Is that right?'

'Aye.' A weary look came into his face, a look that said he'd gone all over this with White's and doubtless other bankers who'd tried to talk clever before and none of them really understood it but even if they did it wouldn't help much, and it was obvious to anyone in the trade, you only had to look at the market statistics: tufteds and needlefelts were growing while woven carpets were virtually stagnating, at least as far as European production was concerned.

'The big development push has been in electronics—things like patterning equipment, quite apart from computers in measurement and automation?'

'I suppose so.'

I smiled. 'You suppose so? Isn't a major part of the rationale behind the amalgamation of you and the Janssens and Rossignol, the pooling of your computer and electronic developments?'

'Mmm—it's a part of it, yes. But rationalizing the product range would be a big part, too.'

'Of course. As with any merger or takeover. But the extra here, the icing on the cake if you like, was that your and Janssens' development should fit with Tapis Rossignol's. Isn't that right?'

He sighed. 'You bankers like everything simple, don't you? Industrial life is never that easy, Tim. But in principle, yes.'

'And Martens was responsible for some experiments at Wingles that you were all gathering to discuss?'

'I'm afraid so.'

'Does it mean that it's all been lost? Whatever development it was?'

He shook his head. 'I don't know. I'll have to go into all that in detail with our research and development people.'

'Ah. Maybe it would help if I could meet someone too. Who is in charge of R & D here?'

'Our R & D division isn't here,' he said. 'It's over at one of the other mills. In Preston.'

'Preston? I see. Who's the man to talk to there?'

'One of my nephews.' He faced me straight, as though defending the implied nepotism of a relative retaining control over something as technical as R & D. 'Brilliant boy, he is. Science degree.' Pride entered his tones. 'From Oxford.'

'Oxford?'

'Aye. My nephew took a science degree at Oxford. He's

my brother's boy—the brother that got it in the second war. RAF, Ted was, Bomber Command, a Lancaster pilot, and I've always been close. Only ten years between us, you see. Done a marvellous job, he has. He's a dab hand with computers, is our Philip.'

'Good heavens.'

'What's up?'

'He's not a dab hand at sailing as well, by any chance?'

Jack Ashworth's battered face crooked into a genial smile. He picked up the thick plate of shortbread biscuits and stuck them under my nose with an inviting gesture.

'I told them you were never a front row man,' he said, cheerfully. 'You're much too quick for a prop.'

4

I caught a late Manchester shuttle and was home to our flat in Onslow Gardens by half past ten. Quite a long day, what with being shown round the mill and eating a hearty lunch, and trying to work out why some carpets have jute backing—that's easy really, it's a question of price—and some have non-wovens, or latex, or foam, and why stability is important, but no one really knows what it is, and how contract carpeting and tiles might use polyester backing or woven polypropylene but usually latex or jute and on and on until my head was spinning. You can only take in so much at a time.

I spoke to Philip Ashworth on the phone but he was just leaving Preston for France and I made an appointment to see him there after he'd had a chance to talk to his un-scorched opposite numbers and someone from Janssens. He sounded rather reserved, perhaps a bit hunted, and I didn't mention Jeremy in case it wasn't tactful or something, but I was going to tell Jeremy that I would be seeing Philip Ashworth, you bet I was.

My wife Sue was sitting up in bed with her tortoiseshell hornrims on, reading a new volume on the reductive approach to minimalist and conceptual art in relation to the use of new materials in the redefinition of traditional iconography. We live sophisticated lives, Sue and I, she being a Curator at the Tate Gallery who likes simple expla-nations of where our income comes from and I being a merchant bank's business consultant who simply likes to know what he's looking at when he sees a painting. So, unlike Jack Sprat and his wife, neither of us is ever quite satisfied. This keeps the marriage lively.

'Hello, Tim,' she said, putting down her book and taking off the glasses. 'Home at last! Have you eaten and everything?'

'Oh yes,' I assured her. 'I've eaten. And everything. Would you like a drink?'

'No, thanks,' she said, cocking her head to look at me, half-sideways. 'How did it go?'

'Not bad,' I said, going off to get myself a dilute whisky, then undressing and washing and getting in beside her.

'Are you very tired?' she asked, turning to me. Her brown hair, unloosed, fell on either side of her face and her blue eyes, large and dark-lashed, looked at me intently.

'A bit. But quite stimulated, really.'

'Stimulated?' She put her hand on mine.

That was the fatal thing, that hand. Up to then I had been going to ask her all about Nevinson and war painters and whether the Nashes were better, or even perhaps Orpen but not Augustus John, and maybe Munnings or Wadsworth or Mark Gertler's fantastic merry-go-round but it stopped me dead in my tracks, did that hand—the Lancashire vernacular is infectious. Because the hand was warm and promising and squeezed ever so slightly, so that its own seemingly disembodied purpose and character communicated a wealth of meaning and promise which would have been instantly terminated if I'd asked the question. Sue would, straight away, have assumed that an interest in Nevinson and war paintings would lead me to trouble and she'd have shot upright and put those hornrimmed glasses back on again and become interrogational.

The last thing I wanted.

So I set aside all the good intentions I had about asking her opinions and put my own pleasures first, before my work, which was reprehensible and irresponsible but man cannot live by work alone, at least that's my excuse; you can work out your own for yourself. I folded Sue tenderly into my arms and let matters take their course but I did wonder, at the back of my mind, why it was I had a nagging worry about shrewd old Jack Ashworth, and his tatty appearance in France, and his feigned ignorance, then, about Robert Graves.

I worried, too, whether he had lied to me all along about that Nevinson, and his grandfather, and the East Lancashire Regiment or, as they were locally known, the Accrington Pals.

Who were massacred on the Somme in July 1916.

Before Nevinson's exhibition took place.

5

'*La réstructurisation de l'industrie de tapis,*' the lugubrious voice of the French squeaker said by way of introduction, '*fait partie de l'objectif de nos investigations statistiques—*'

This was going to take hours. I don't know why it is that the Frogs love formal perorations, but they do. Something Napoleon bequeathed to them, perhaps.

'*Auprès du marché français des revêtements de sols—*'

We were sitting in the formal meeting-room, a minor *grand salon*, in the elegant eighteenth-century premises of Maucourt Frères, not far from the Elysée Palace on the Rue du Faubourg Saint-Honoré. Just off the Faubourg, in fact, but part of that splendid atmosphere. At the head of the long table Eugène Maucourt, the gelid operational chief of the Maucourt Frères investment bank, sat rigidly upright, appearing to listen intently. The exposition was going through something of a checklist on flooring. France is not a major producer or consumer of carpets; the French are still very fond of parquet and ceramic tiles, not to mention linoleum.

'*Parquets traditionnels,*' the squeaker intoned, '*grès émaille pressé, revêtements vinyliques—feuilles et dalles—*'

The man next to Eugène Maucourt started picking his nose. He was dressed, to Maucourt's evident displeasure, in a bristly grey herringbone sports coat and brown flannels, exactly what you might expect a tufted carpet manufacturer from the back streets of Lille and Roubaix to wear on a day out to Paris. He had stiff black hair swept straight back from his head and a stiff black moustache, thick as a brush, swept down straight under his nose, from whose nostrils black hair also bristled. Opposite him, in a brown striped

suit, rather more elegant, but challenged by a cream shirt
with dotted brown diamond motifs, sat Tapis Rossignol's
manager from Vierzon, south of Orléans, whence regional
development funds had lured Rossignol in a new factory
venture. Next to them sat, on each side, first a finance man
from Rossignol's Paris office and secondly one of the heavy
mob from Roubaix, who looked as though he was there to
duff someone up. An uglier, more broken-nosed, barrel-
chested minder I had never seen in my life.

'*Le Syndicat Français des Enducteurs et Calandreurs Fabricants
Revêtements de Sols et Murs*—'

The squeaker's problem, as everyone probably knew, was
that the Belgians are the biggest producers of carpets in
Western Europe and the Germans and the British have the
biggest markets. France may be a leader of fashion but its
textile industry ain't quite as hot. As a producer, the dear
old UK comes second to Belgium and ahead of West Germany. We do love carpeting our floors wall to wall, a bit
like the Yanks.

'*L'Union Européene de la Meublement à Bruxelles*—'

The poor squeaker really had been covering the ground,
he really had. He wasn't a bad chap, called Jaques Charville, one of Eugène Maucourt's up-and-coming kinder-
garten of select École Whatsitsname graduates, but he was
a bit overawed. Opposite me, for instance, Sir Richard
White cast his grey patrician shadow across the table. Next
to me, between me and the squeaker, the superbly-suited
figure of the great entrepreneur Jean Malfait, effective
owner of Tapis Rossignol and one of France's leading industrialists, smoked a pensive cigarette, extracted from an
initialled case which somehow conveyed the knowledge that
the cigarettes were specially blended for him. He it was
who had put together four factories—Roubaix, Wingles,
Vierzon and a smaller one at Lens, not represented here—
to form the enterprise known as Tapis Rossignol—Nightin-

gale Carpets—who had thus become, willy-nilly, clients of
Maucourt Frères due to Malfait's long association with the
family and bank.

'*L'Union des Fabricants de Tapis de France à Neuville-en-
Ferrain*—'

Malfait, I supposed, would have his own lines of com-
munication to all these industry committees, trade associ-
ations and the like but here we were, pledged to play this
official game, step this ritual galliard, so that everyone
could be satisfied that professional steps had been taken,
proper consultation carried out, economic and environmen-
tal analysis weighed up, employment implications assessed
and adjudged. Things which I had assumed were all well
under way when I'd been called across to Wingles.

'*Tapis touffetés vis-à-vis tapis à points noués ou, plus important,
aiguilletés, nappés, tricotés, flockés*—'

He was making heavy weather of it. The black-brush-
moustached tufter from Roubaix squeezed his nose again,
pensively, as though considering whether to pick it a bit
deeper in or to have an exploratory blast on his handker-
chief. The ugly minder, catching me looking at his chief
and obviously inattentive, gave me a surprising, startling
wink. It was rather like having a pit bull lick your hand: I
winked faintly back, more in shock-reaction than anything
else.

Charville paused to get his breath and took a swig of
mineral water to lubricate his dry throat.

'Splendid,' Sir Richard chimed in. 'An excellent *tour
d' horizon*.'

Charville looked startled, glass in hand. He was only just
getting into his stride. The faces of the rest of them flicked
and resettled, looking more in hope than curiosity at Sir
Richard.

'I'm sure—' Sir Richard's French was impeccable but
I'm not going to tire you with it— 'that we all much

appreciate this restatement of the background to the negotiations which are being conducted. The stability of the European market for carpets and the effect of socio-economic
pressures and long-term fashions must be taken into account. Population may be stable or even declining but
the number of households is growing. And so on and so
forth.'

I stifled a smile. You can rubbish market research by
picking on one minor error or you can wave away an entire
panorama as irrelevant. Sir Richard looked to be about to
take the second course. He wasn't going to be tactless
enough to remind his audience that France's residential
living area is scarcely half that of West Germany or make
demographic jokes about bathrooms, the French, soap and
perfume. He was just going to put the boot in on the market
research for the moment because he wanted to get down to
business, other business, that was obviously occupying his
mind.

'What we need—' Sir Richard's smooth assurance made
the way he ignored Charville's disconcerted expression
seem quite logical—'is to concentrate our minds on the way
in which a much larger, more competitive grouping can be
established. I do not need to remind anyone here of the
enormous size of Beaulieu in Belgium, the sheer scale of
their operations and vertical integration, to make it obvious
that those who wish to survive in this industry, especially
after 1992, will need to form much bigger groupings. Trans-
European groupings. The EIU report, for example, makes
it quite clear that West Germany has higher weaving costs
but, when landed costs are considered, it is almost as competitive as others. The developed economies of Western
Europe have moved to encourage the industry to re-equip,
to go in for high quality, capital intensive goods and to
invest heavily to use the advances made in computer technology.' He paused to let the words sink in before repeating

them. 'Computer technology, gentlemen. We are not here, therefore, to discuss the *whether* of our situation. We are here to discuss *how*. And to get on with that how quickly.'

That did it. Poor Charville never stood a chance after that. They all tried to speak at once but, being French and sitting in the surroundings they were in, position prevailed. The head of the table was soon in lone peroration while they listened respectfully.

'One cannot but agree with Sir Richard.' Eugène Maucourt's oratorical style made it sound as though his agreement came with the greatest regret. 'The economies of scale impose restructuring of an essential order, particularly in the application of expensive, centralized computer technology.'

I found myself frowning slightly. The days when you had to build a computer the size of a battleship, housed in a reinforced concrete building in a vast central armoury, are long gone. The flexibility of modern computer hardware, the neatness of small but powerful terminals, swept all that away. The software and its application, though, is another matter. You can blow a fortune on that. What Eugène Maucourt was getting at, I supposed, was that as usual the French was bidding for the centralized systems to be based in France, not anywhere else.

'The example Sir Richard has cited—that of Beaulieu Tufting, etcetera—is one which doubtless preoccupies us all. That company accounts for about—what? forty per cent of Belgian tufted carpet production?' He raised his lofty eyebrows at Charville who, pathetically grateful at being restored to the conversation, nodded excitedly. 'Forty per cent,' Eugène Maucourt repeated, looking from face to face significantly, as though he'd just brought a rabbit out of his hat. 'Forty per cent of the biggest national production in Europe, concentrated in one company. The economies of scale have been highly beneficial. Beaulieu's utilization of nylon yarns is so extensive that it has gone into production on its own. It has set up its own primary backing production in Polyweave, to make the woven polypropylene materials required.'

He paused at this point, looking satisfied at his own exposition, which doubtless, after intensive briefing by Charville, was intended to show his client just how *au fait* with events in the European carpet industry he was. Facts at his fingertips, and all that crap. Malfait took another smooth pull on one of his elegant cigarettes and, with a curious movement of his eyebrows, up and down, signified approbation and assent.

'If, to these benefits—' encouraged, Eugène Maucourt raised his left forearm to an angle of forty-five degrees, hand open, in much the manner of the late General De Gaulle —'is added a computer systems facility of a revolutionary new order, the competitive benefits would be intense. It is, one does not have to emphasize, an absolute necessity for carpet producers who wish to survive in the future. Such producers would, as Sir Richard has pointed out, need to be established on a trans-national basis in order to obtain the maximum benefit in terms of distribution costs as well as economies of scale and vertical integration.'

The French do love an intellectual challenge. They really do. I could imagine some geezer with his computer glowing red hot, spectacles steaming up, churning out the optimum locations for a series of carpet factories in Europe, taking into account the different types of product and the concentration of demand in each area or zone or city, to come up with a vast, memory-blowing plan detailed down to the last looper and picker, only to find that one of the factories would have to be placed on the site of the Eiffel Tower. Mind you, that wouldn't upset a Frenchman in the least. He would have shown, beyond all challenge, that the prob-

lem had been solved with rigorous theoretical and intellectual efficiency.

In the meantime the Germans would be researching lab-
oratory production of higher yield monofilament yarns by
new petrochemical research; the Belgians would be belting
out lower cost broadlooms; the Italians would be fudging
their production statistics in order to salt funds away in
Switzerland; and the British would be swearing and cursing
about lorry delays at Dover ferry car park. People never
change.

'Sir Richard—' Jean Malfait's voice, now that he suddenly spoke up, was deep, very masculine— 'and you,
Eugène, have undoubtedly a firm grasp of the principles
which must guide any conjuncture which takes place between ourselves, Louis Janssens, and—' he made a slight
nod in Sir Richard's direction—'our English friends, who
have expressed an enthusiasm for this venture.'

He made the last bit sound very condescending, as
though 'our English friends' were people teeming beyond
an emotionally conceptual barrier to the north, not just a
physical barrier like the Channel. An enthusiasm is not
enthusiasm, either; as with the Common Market and so on,
the enthusiasm of the English had little credibility in these
surroundings. I caught Sir Richard's eye on me but he
needn't have worried; I was behaving myself impeccably,
just like a tailor's dummy stuffed into a Regent Street suit.

'It is very important—' Malfait's tone deepened to
express a commitment to his words—'that the recent unfortunate events at Wingles do not retard the programme we
have established for the negotiations. As Sir Richard has
said, it is not whether but how. And the how must be done
quickly.'

He looked challengingly round the table, as though there
might be someone present, apart from Sir Richard and me,
who would provide an objection. Since the others depended

on him for a living in some way or another he didn't get one. They all nodded sagely, taking words like 'unfortunate events' in their stride. Sir Richard put on an expression of approval.

'Excellent,' he said, clearly. 'Excellent. I am glad we are all in agreement. After such distressing events it is well for basic principles and objectives to be re-stated. My colleague, Mr Simpson, has just arrived from Lancashire. We are proceeding to Belgium immediately after this meeting. No effort, therefore, is being spared by Maucourt Frères—' he inclined a head gracefully at Eugène—'or, need I say, White's Bank, to expedite this matter. We are fully aware, you may be assured, of the importance to all concerned.'

He raised his eyebrows slightly in interrogation at Malfait, who had turned just a fraction to look at me. Malfait nodded slowly.

'Mr Simpson will now be handling the English side?' he queried.

'Together with me, yes.' Sir Richard was unperturbed. 'We have decided that an extra resource will help speed things up.'

Malfait nodded again, his eyes going beyond me to Eugène Maucourt.

'Mr Simpson has worked with us before.' Eugène Maucourt didn't sound wildly enthusiastic, but a little warmth seeped into his voice. 'We have collaborated with excellent results.'

Malfait stopped his nodding, seeming to be satisfied. I wondered what grimy secrets he and Eugène concealed between them, what awful discretion was going to be necessary, then closed my mind. They wouldn't involve me if they could avoid it and I didn't want to know.

The meeting broke up, Eugène shaking hands with me and Sir Richard before escorting Malfait off to his private sanctum. The squeaker, Jacques Charville, nipped across the room to nobble me with an appealing smile.

'Tim! Good to see you. So you are joining us?'

'Hello, Jacques. I've been roped in, you might say.'

'Oh, good. Thank heavens you're here. I haven't put forward half the figures. Sir Richard intervened at the crucial point. You see—'

He stopped. A vast bulk had heaved alongside. The great pug-ugly from Roubaix breathed down on Charville and then put his face into mine as though about to bite my nose off. Disconcerted, I peered at him.

'*Tu ne me rappelles pas?*' he asked, his face splitting into a terrible grin. '*A Lille? Rugby? C'est toi, Tim? Le même Simpson?*'

'Good God! Kolewski? François Kolewski?'

He burst into a roar of laughter. 'Not bad! But your memory's going, eh? Like mine!'

'You played flanker for Lille! I remember you, now!'

'Got it!'

He embraced me fit to split seams. Kolewski was a horrifically powerful rugby player, a descendant of the Polish immigration to northern French coal mines. My tours in France with scratch British sides had made me a lot of pals ten years ago; evenings lost in a beery haze blurred the faces, the broken noses like mine, the vast aggressive grins of men you'd tried to stop in mud-churning collisions. Kolewski had been prominent among them.

'Small world, eh?'

'You bet!'

'Hell, François, I'm sorry I haven't time for a beer and a yarn with you. I've got to run with Sir Richard.'

'Sure. Next time, eh? You'll be in Roubaix, for sure.' He winked broadly and jerked his head towards the table where we had been sitting. 'If that's anything to go by.' His beam took in Charville, who gaped at us anxiously. 'Won't he, Jacques?'

'Er, yes.' Charville looked nervous. 'I'm sure. But when can we meet, Tim?'

I had to think briefly, wondering what secrets Eugène Maucourt's tame researcher would want to share with me.

'I'll be back in two or three days,' I said. 'That do?'

He nodded briskly, smiled nervously at Kolewski, and left. I found myself staring after him.

'Tell me—' I lowered my voice—'what the hell was all that about?'

Kolewski's smile broadened a little, then faded. 'Bullshit, Tim. *Merde*. That's what that was about.' His eye moved to where his boss, the black-moustachioed nose-picker was standing, smiling towards us and moving his head better to listen. Kolewski's voice went louder, making sure he could hear. 'Come and see us, Tim, when you're through with Janssens. We'll remind you of what good beer is like, eh?'

'That'd be great.'

'Sure.'

He clapped me on the back and indicated the doorway, where Sir Richard was making it obvious he was waiting. His voice dropped as he moved in that direction with me.

'Take care, Tim. *C'est un terrain brûlant, tu connais?*'

I nodded at the pun without replying, seeing Sir Richard's face too patiently regarding me from the doorway. If it weren't dangerous ground, I remember thinking —burning ground, in French—he wouldn't have brought me over in the first place.

6

Sir Richard White drove the Jaguar saloon skilfully out to the Porte Maillot and then round the *périphérique* to the north to take the A1 to Lille. We were soon past Charles de Gaulle airport and through the first *péage*.

'Penny for them,' he said, after a while. 'You were uncharacteristically silent at our meeting, Tim, for which I was grateful, and are so now, for which I am not.'

'Nothing there. Blank mind.'

'Rubbish.'

I grinned. 'I was waiting for you to tell me what all this is about.'

'Come, come. You know that. It's a merger between three companies. One Belgian, one British, one French. A lot of capital could be committed, very soon. Question of survival. What did you think of Ashworth's place?'

'Very interesting. Modern equipment inside an old setting. Exterior appearance misleading. Like Ashworth himself.'

He smiled significantly. 'Very good. Go on.'

'Darwen is only one mill. There's a bigger one at Preston. Makes a mixture of tufted and woven carpets. Another at Warrington, which is nearly all needlefelt contract carpeting, including tiles. More profitable than domestic stuff.'

'So they say. I'm not disputing it just now, either. But I haven't been to that mill.'

'The R & D section is at Preston and Jeremy's college chum Philip, the Oxford sailor, is the nephew in charge of it.'

'Precisely. I gather you were unable to persuade Jeremy to join you in your visit?'

'I'm afraid not.'

There was a silence. The sign for Compiègne had come and gone, the green countryside peeling past us at ninety miles an hour in the Jaguar's effortless cruise.

'That's a pity.' Sir Richard didn't sound very upset. 'I believe that Jeremy hasn't seen Philip Ashworth for a long time and is, understandably, a little shy of barging in, so to speak, but this is a major project and we are in need of clarification. Everything we can get. I will have to see him on my next visit to London. It's essential.'

'Mmm.' I could imagine that dialogue and made a mental note to be somewhere else when it took place.

'You must help me to persuade him.' Sir Richard's intuitions were always remorselessly accurate. 'You and he are so close. He sets great store by your views.'

You old buzzard, I thought. So that's it: I've been brought in to persuade Jeremy. A sort of mole.

'Not that that's the main reason, of course, why I am calling upon your illustrious services in this case.'

'Oh?'

'Come, come, Tim. You've gone all monosyllabic on me. Let's hear it. What do you think about this proposed merger?'

'Well—' the sign for Péronne came up on the right. Then another: *Champ de Bataille de la Somme*. Christ. There was no getting away from something to do with 1914–18 in this affair. Ashworths and Robert Graves and the Somme, here they were again; it was coming back to me.

'Yes? You seem a bit distrait, if I may say so.' Sir Richard's patience was wearing thin. There was a time, not long ago, when he would have been much more acerbic, but after a couple of false starts he and I had become friends. In a way he had a rather paternal attitude to me and felt it was his duty to draw me away from Jeremy's anarchic presence to a place under his own wing where, given good

behaviour, my career might prosper in a wider sphere than
that of Gracechurch Street. Which was very kind of him
but left difficulties with Jeremy, old loyalties to cosset as
one tried to temper the new, chillier breezes emanating from
Europe to the shorn lamb of British investment banking. Sir
Richard was anxious to develop business on the Continent
and had created a place for me in doing this, but I still had
obligations to Jeremy that were indissolubly close.

It was putting me in a difficult position.

As the actress said to the bishop.

'Tell me, Richard.' I managed to marshal my thoughts.
'Whose idea was this merger in the first place?'

'Is that important?' He was beginning to sound a bit
testy.

'To me, yes. I'd like to know who was the prime motivator.'

'Fair enough, Tim. I suppose it was Malfait and Eugène
Maucourt. They got in touch with Janssens because Malfait, quite logically, thought that a tie-up with the Belgians
made sense.'

'So how did Ashworth come into it?'

He smiled. 'I brought Ashworth into it. We had a routine
meeting in Paris when Eugène reported what was going on,
and in my capacity as European co-ordinator I thought of
the Dillworth Carpet Company, for whom White's have
acted for many years. Our policy nowadays is to think
European for our clients. Why not?'

'Why not, of course. The fees might be much bigger. But
I can't see why Janssens doesn't simply expand without
getting involved with other companies.'

Combles would soon come up on our left. Beyond Combles it was all British cemeteries, dozens of them, out to
Thiepval and on up to Arras.

'A good question, Tim. But expansion requires capital.

And concentration in Belgium alone begs the distribution question, doesn't it?'

'Yes, Richard. Especially as far as Britain is concerned.'

Just about five miles away, still over to our left, would be Mametz, shown shelled to ruins in *Goodbye To All That* and, nearby, the two Bazentin villages between which, in 1916, Robert Graves was so badly perforated by shell splinters that his mother was sent an official letter regretting his decease.

'Precisely, Tim. So you see the argument for Janssens and Dillworth carpets getting together?'

The Von Ranke strain was tough. Graves survived even though he'd been written off, and went on to write those books and all that poetry. He was barmy about women, of course, hadn't the faintest idea, but you could put all that down to his school and his religious German mother.

'Er, yes. That's what I thought, too. They don't really need Tapis Rossignol at all, strategically. Quite an interesting intervention of yours, Richard.'

Just to the west of the Bazentins the minor river called the Ancre, before it flows into Albert, divides the terrible killing ground around Beaumont Hamel, where in July 1916 the East Lancashires were mown down in rows. The famous monument by Lutyens at Thiepval stands above the whole awful scene.

'That's just it, Tim. You've put your finger on it.'

The sign for Bapaume came up ahead. Of course! That famous desolate painting of the awful empty road going endlessly over the naked bumps of devastated country. Of course! My thoughts clicked into place at last. *The Road from Arras to Bapaume*. Nevinson! Who else? Now I had linked Nevinson, and Robert Graves, and the Ashworths, all here together. It was getting more than distracting; I had to make an effort to go on.

'I mean, Richard, quite honestly, Tapis Rossignol is a

bit of a hotch-potch put together by Malfait with French
Government assistance in one of his obscure entrepreneurial deals. Probably as a favour to some minister in
return for a bigger boatful of gravy somewhere else. It
doesn't look very good in the figures I've seen. Not what
you'd call a hot property at all.'

'Now you seem more animated. And, if you'll excuse me,
typically British. You can find reasons for combining with
a Belgian company, whose profit record isn't all that hot
either, but not with a French one, whose situation is a bit
similar to Dillworth's. And you assume some sort of dirty
work at official level in France. A rather insular view.'

'Who needs another Dillworth's? Janssens has an integrated factory of large size concentrated in one strategic
location instead of three or four mills scattered about the
place. Of varying age and suitability for modern manufac-
ture. And there's bound to be dirty work at official level in
France. The Common Market is all about interventionist,
dirigiste politics with gravy trains attached for regional
deputies and mayors and the whole bloody gang. It's been
natural to them for decades. Centuries, even. People don't
change.'

'My dear Tim! Now you are getting very animated! And
extremely prejudiced. Political corruption hasn't been confined only to the Continent, you know. Nor backhanders of
all sorts.'

I shut my mouth. Arras was coming up on our left. The
autoroute would sweep east of Lens, south of Lille, then
we'd be on the A17 to Courtrai. The old road, the N17
from Arras to Bapaume that Nevinson painted, was almost
parallel to us, only three or four miles distant, but we were
sealed off from it like travellers in future space from a trade
route on the old Earth's ocean.

'Concentration in one place isn't necessarily the answer.'
Unlike me, Sir Richard had been doing his homework and

wasn't distracted by suspicions, historical or biographical details and connections, the clutter of a mind like mine. 'There's an economic size for each type of production line, each form of carpet, that isn't infinitely large or fast. You know that, Tim. All sorts of limitations apply. A blend of different sizes of factory is almost certainly the answer.'

'Which is what Ashworth has got with the Dillworth Carpet Company.' I had my answer ready for that one.

'In Lancashire. But you're right. Which is why you put your finger on it when you said that strategically Rossignol isn't absolutely necessary. Of course one always aims, in taking over another company, to buy its clients and good-will and so on. If you can get them at the right price you gain easy access to wider markets. But Malfait has priced Rossignol well above that.'

'Because of Martens' work?'

We had left the fields of the Somme behind. Industrial Lens to one side and Douai the other heralded the approach to Lille, that Manchester of France, with its clustering satellites of Roubaix and Tourcoing, like Salford and Oldham, clinging to its north-eastern skirts. The Jaguar began to slow down.

'Martens and others. Some sort of major computer systems work that would make an impact technologically and on efficiencies in several areas. Martens had given papers on the subject at various technical symposiums—sorry, symposia—without, of course, giving too much away. Both Janssens and Ashworth were very interested. The proposed new group had been talked about anyway, between them only and in confidence, of course, but the combination of their own computer work and Rossignol's got them excited. There's no point in each company separately trying to invent the wheel; pooling their resources is an obvious move.'

'So we're stuck with Malfait as the original motivator and the meeting with Martens was fairly crucial.'

'Exactly.'

'I'm not sure, then, why you sent for me. Wouldn't a computer freak of some kind have been more appropriate?'

Sir Richard White smiled slightly as he slowed down a bit more to negotiate the dog-leg from the A1 across to the A17. 'Not really. You see, two nights before the meeting, one late afternoon at Maucourt's in fact, Martens phoned me at my office there. He was speaking from Wingles, I think, and he seemed distraught. He knew Maucourt Frères were acting as brokers in this thing—Maucourt's being Malfait's advisers for years and we Ashworth's—but he said he felt he could trust me. I was surprised. I'd only met him once, quite normally, on a visit to the factory at Wingles with Eugène, when we first started preparing the dossier. A pleasant enough man, bit technical of course, you know how these computer men are, but managerially competent. I didn't try to impress him particularly. Eugène was more the contact with Rossignol than me, obviously. I was to handle the Dillworth side.'

No wonder, I thought, Jeremy was a bit nettled. No one thought to involve him until they got into difficulties. If all had gone to plan, the kudos would have been Sir Richard's and Eugène's; complications and difficulties like the fire had led to Jeremy being asked to join in, to share the risk.

Like me, for instance.

'Martens spoke hurriedly, saying he was short of time. He said it would be impossible to meet before Ashworth and Janssens arrived. But he was not insistent that we talk privately after our meeting. He said it was about a very important matter, one that might place him in personal danger.'

'Did he say what sort of danger?'

'No. He rang off hurriedly. I was upset. And in a quandary. I didn't want to alarm or disturb Eugène Maucourt, or to breach a confidentiality. I must say I was at a bit of a loss. The thought that there might be danger alarmed me, never mind the thought of alarming Eugène; you know what he's like. Martens had seemed such a normal sort of man. I mean normal for a computer technician, of course, because they're so impossible to pin down. Never give you a straight answer. So uncommercial. Hedge everything they say and try to blind you with science.' Sir Richard shrugged as far as driving would allow him to shrug, as if to shake off the memory of the inexplicable ways of technical men, and brightened perceptibly. 'The solution, at least a temporary one, came to me naturally. I sent for you.'

'Thank you, Richard.' I tried not to sound too dry.

'When you arrived so precisely I was mightily relieved. Everything seemed to be in better order. Even Bob Janssens' little diversion delaying us didn't make me impatient, although my instinct was to get to Wingles a bit early. Then the fire.' He shook his head before glancing sideways as we fed into a fast lane after a junction. 'That terrible fire. It's too coincidental, Tim. There's nothing left of Martens and I bet the assessors'll be short of evidence. Too much destruction. The heat! It was shocking.'

'Mmm. Have you told anyone else about Martens' call to you?'

'Not a soul.'

We were skirting the eastern edge of Lille and Roubaix, with Courtrai, or Kortrijk if you're Flemish, signposted ahead. You can flit in and out of France and Belgium at ease, crossing the border like running in and out of Lancashire and Yorkshire. None of that Dover-ferry, anything-to-declare nonsense. No Customs & Excise men in dark uniforms hinting that you may have a bomb or a rabid fox in your boot. It's been like that for donkey's years. Mind you, insularity isn't confined to the British; if you speak in

French to a Fleming he often won't answer. Much prefers to use English if you can't speak his own impossible language; there's no love lost between Fleming and Frenchman.

'The fact of the matter is that Martens' death makes me highly suspicious. But why, and what benefit there might be to someone in all these negotiations is something to which we are going to have to bend our minds.' Sir Richard White gestured at a sign ahead. 'Ah, here we are, entering Belgium. The cockpit of Europe, Tim.'

7

It turned out that Bob Janssens possessed a mistress and more than one suit. The other suit was a check twill of the sort that Jeeves would have allowed Bertie Wooster to wear for a spring morning's walk in the park but not for formal occasions. It was an English cloth probably tailored in Switzerland or even Italy, where businessmen all seem to have given up suits in order to wear tweed sports jackets and dark grey flannels, like public schoolboys let out at half term. The Belgians tend to think of themselves as cosmopolitan but Janssens was definitely Anglophile that morning; the steel-grey image had softened into an off-duty gentleman's.

The mistress wasn't introduced as such, of course, nothing so indiscreet. She was titled Marketing Director, but I can spot 'em a mile off. She was tall, blonde, very attentive to Sir Richard and slightly appraising of me while smiling a wide white smile of welcome. I caught an amused glint in my employer's eye but no more; the old buzzard has been all the way there and back. Janssens made a pretty good fist of presenting her—Elizabeth van Laeten was her name—and how she co-ordinated all the marketing effort and was a textile designer and knew the European business backwards and so on, but it was a lost cause. She was the best bit of soft furniture in the place and it all belonged to Janssens, you really got that message straight away.

Sir Richard and I had spent a night at a hotel off the Grand Market in Courtrai, quite modest but with the usual excellent restaurant; I've never eaten badly in Belgium. The Janssens factory was on the south side of town, heading back towards Tourcoing. It was an ultra-modern place, a great white box of a building going deeply back off the main road towards some railway sidings and a jumble of older buildings. In front of it a small garden of evergreens was neatly clipped round a circular pool with the Belgian, French and EEC flags ranged on a line of posts. We entered a panelled foyer with presentation showcases of multi-coloured carpets spread in a collage on one wall and thick books of swatches piled strategically on tables beside arm-chairs for visitors. The specifications were all printed in English, French, Dutch, German, Italian and Spanish; our coffee came in German bone china, not railway pottery.

When we got into Bob Janssens' office it was nothing like Ashworth's either. It was very clean and modern, with teak and steel furniture, except for a large antique Low Coun-tries bureau-bookcase against one wall, a huge Flemish oak affair with a Dutch gable up top, a glazed astragal-moulded bookcase full of books, and a bureau that was so bombé it curved in all pot-bellied directions, as though the cabinet maker had been accused of an inability to work in three dimensions and was out to refute the charge. The chairs we sat in were moulded plywood à la Charles Eames, buttoned black leather upholstery, very comfortable and fashionably 'fifties in style. The carpet was a beige cut pile velour with a formal printed line and border panelled to fit the room. Very impressive; the carpet trade was doing all right in these parts.

'A dreadful business,' Janssens was saying to Sir Richard. 'Horrible. Really horrible. I didn't know Martens well, of course, just from business acquaintance and our discussions over these last few months, but well enough to feel person-ally affected.' He lowered his voice respectfully. 'There is virtually nothing left, apparently. It complicates the official procedures enormously.' He gave us a meaningful look. 'You know what the French are like.'

We nodded sympathetically; of course we knew what the French are like.

'Depositions from people who last saw Martens alive inside the works, that sort of thing. Statements all over. Technical evidence. Ashes.' Janssens' face crinkled. 'Tests for human minerals. Grisly. The French seem to enjoy it.'

We nodded again in solidarity. I couldn't think of any country which wouldn't require depositions from witnesses and tests among the ashes for phosphorus or whatever it would be that human combustibles would leave behind, but the French could be indicted with a lamentably enjoyed fussiness in such matters. It gave us British and Belgians a measure of comradeship.

'Really—' Elizabeth van Laeten's voice was attractively husky as she joined in on the subject—'one would feel terribly for his family—I mean nothing, absolutely nothing, left to bury. Pre-cremated, you might say. As it happens, it seems there isn't any close family in that sense. He wasn't married.'

'Ah.' Sir Richard hit the right note of interest and mild relief. 'In that case it is perhaps providential.'

'Indeed.' Janssens nodded emphatically. 'There'll be a memorial service, of course, which Malfait is organizing as a mark of respect to his late employee, but at least there won't be distraught relatives and so on. At least I haven't heard of any. As Elizabeth says, it would be terrible for them. Like a wartime loss, really.'

'Quite so.' Sir Richard knows more about wartime losses than most, but nothing in his tone implied any special knowledge. 'Apart from the, er, the human questions, do you think that the fire will raise complicated demands from assessors, insurance authorities and the police?'

Janssens pulled a face. 'A fire like that does no one any good. It makes people check on regulations all over Europe. All those materials are present here in our own factory. We do everything we can towards security, of course, but there are limits in any manufacturing process. As I understand it, there is no evidence yet on how the fire started.' He smiled significantly. 'The insurance people will not be very happy about that.'

'Oh?'

Elizabeth van Laeten gave Sir Richard a dazzling smile. 'The equipment at Wingles was pretty out of date. A suspicious mind might imply that it has been rather convenient to be rid of it that way.'

Sir Richard pulled a long lip. He'd been to Wingles before, as he'd said, but he couldn't be expected to know too much about carpet production lines. Eugène Maucourt would know the book depreciation, though, which would reveal the age of the equipment.

'Surely,' I asked, 'if Wingles was where Martens was doing his computer work, shouldn't the machinery have been fairly up to date?'

'Ah.' Elizabeth van Laeten crossed a long leg over another and smiled at me from behind an elegantly raised knee. 'That's the point. It was easier to carry out experiments on the older, slower equipment than to interrupt production on the faster lines at Roubaix and Vierzon. Martens could do his work with more facility at Wingles and prove it there before it could be put on the newer lines. If it worked at Wingles, it was sure to work in the other places.'

That didn't seem necessarily to follow, but Janssens anticipated any query I might have made. 'There was a close collaboration, of course, between the different factories. Some parts of Martens' systems were tried at Roubaix. Patterning equipment in particular. I would guess that everything Martens designed was intended for new equipment but worked in principle on the old as well.' He smiled at his marketing director. 'An older system can work just as successfully on a younger application.'

Her eyes hooded briefly and her mouth twitched. Sir Richard and I smiled politely to show that we had got the joke. I saw Janssens' expression glow with possessive humour as he stared at her. His rich brown tan was suffused with pink and his muscular frame shifted inside the quiet twill. He was, in many ways, the epitome of the modern European businessman, multi-lingual, probably observant of health, early to work, concerned with efficiency, business logic and rational approaches to living which engendered broad loyalties. For a moment he made me feel insular, rude, subjective of judgement, too densely preoccupied with ancient history, sudden death and cemeteries. Then, seeing that his expression towards his Marketing Director was becoming more than a bit obvious, I hastened to break the significant pause in conversation that had ensued.

'You seem to have a fair idea of what Martens was doing. The full extent of the proposed amalgamation hasn't been settled yet. I don't suppose Martens can have given you too much detailed information?'

Janssens, recollecting himself, grinned. 'Not officially, no. Although Martens was Belgian, of course, and we got on well, so I did perhaps get a bit more information than others might have. But he was loyal to Rossignol; the only other person who understood the thrust of his work was Philip Ashworth, who is here today and who you'll meet shortly. He's talking to my own computer men right now but we'll see him when he's finished. He's agreed to join us here.'

'Splendid.' Sir Richard brightened visibly. 'It will be invaluable, won't it, Tim, to hear from the horse's mouth what all this is about. After poor Martens' er, accident, we need to understand more fully what the implications for a concentration of computer work are likely to be, don't we?'

'Yes.'

My reply must have come out a bit stolidly. He gave me an odd glance, but to me something was starting to smell completely wrong. Either someone was buying a pig in a poke, or someone was having to give away too much before signatures got on to dotted lines and money changed hands. If Malfait was dangling Rossignol's computer developments as bait, and Ashworth was checking into what it all was, and someone had to assess the effect of pooling these resources between three companies, the shadow boxing could become too devious for words. What protection Rossignol had on the imparting information and how much Ashworth and Janssens needed to know before buying, yet without possessing the whole bag of tricks, was something only experts could judge. The proof of the pudding would be in the eating, I supposed; if the systems could be demonstrated in some way on pilot plant equipment or a prototype attached to an existing line, then the contents of the black box of tricks, whatever they were, could be kept secret. The results were what mattered.

'Is there,' I asked Janssens directly, 'a compelling argument for this amalgamation anyway? Without the computer side coming into it?'

'Of course!' He had completely diverted his attention from his blonde executive. 'There's always an argument, in a relatively static or slow-growing market, for combining to gain market share and rationalize on overheads and costs. Especially now that Europe is heading to be one market. You can simply buy your share of France, or the UK, or whatever. It's a matter of price, of course. What price should you pay to buy that share, those assets, those people?' He smiled significantly. 'Many companies have paid too much for such takeovers. Many have gained no significant benefit from their foreign or competitive acquisitions.'

'Mmm.' He didn't have to tell a merchant banker that.

All you have to do is open the business pages of any news-paper to read doleful figures on ham-fisted mergers.

The office door opened and Philip Ashworth came in. We all sprang to our feet. I knew it was him because there was a family resemblance; he had the same eyes and mouth as his uncle. There the similarity ended. He was shorter, thinner and reticent. A shy smile responded to Elizabeth van Laeten's dazzling greeting, a smile which was retained as he was introduced to us and while he avoided our eyes, although he dwelt a fraction longer on my handshake than the others.

'I'm sorry I couldn't see you in Preston,' he murmured. 'I thought I'd better get over here right away.'

'Of course.'

He wore a drab suit of grey and a blue shirt with a red tie. His shoes were a nondescript black. I put him down as older than Jeremy and felt surprised to think that they were contemporaries. He didn't look as though he sailed. He hadn't got an open-air, healthy look like Janssens. His skin was pale and he looked tired.

'We've been very anxious to meet you.' Sir Richard was crisp, getting straight to the point. 'Tim and I hastened here after a meeting to agree objectives in Paris.'

Philip Ashworth nodded and sat down, taking a cup of coffee from Elizabeth van Laeten with a vague smile of thanks. His gaze wandered off Sir Richard for a moment towards Bob Janssens, saw him, avoided his return stare, and looked down into his coffee.

'It is,' Sir Richard continued remorselessly as we all reseated ourselves, 'a matter of the utmost urgency that we talk to you, as we had intended to do with Martens before his awful accident.'

Philip Ashworth nodded and took a sip from his coffee.

'As I'm sure you're aware—' Sir Richard moderated his tone to a slightly more appealing, lower pitch—'the whole question of the final terms hinges on the value placed upon the intangible assets of Rossignol in regard to its computer developments. Your opinion of these assets is very important.'

Ashworth nodded again.

'Is there anything you can tell us at this stage?'

It was as blunt a question as you could get. Ashworth didn't seem surprised. Although he was the antithesis of his uncle you could sense a resolution, a Lancashire doggedness in him, doubtless inherited from generations of moorland and mill-owning Ashworths. He stirred a spoon into his coffee, hesitated, and then spoke indirectly, without looking up, almost as if he were addressing a distant, lecture audience at a technical college.

'The use of computers in the carpet industry—' his voice was low and educated but with just a touch of northern hardness in the vowels— 'has tended to be concentrated in two areas. One is in patterning equipment, where microprocessors control either the yarn dyeing or the printing operations used in the tufting process. A master computer holds the pattern information and then feeds minicomputers at patterning heads along the line. The minicomputers control the introduction of the right coloured yarns at the prescribed points. Or you can record a design, separate out the colours and then control the action of dye jets to produce what you want by printing. These are the patterning applications. The other area of applications is in systems generally to control the whole process of production, materials, stock controls and so on, depending on sales and invoicing as with any factory.'

Sir Richard had managed to follow this. 'Which area was Martens working in?' he demanded. 'Patterning or general systems?'

'Both,' said Philip Ashworth. 'But the interest for us was in patterning. Rossignol have done considerable development along the lines of design printing, rather in the wake of Dynapoint and Kaleidoscopic, but with additions and variations of their own.' He paused to look at the incomprehension on Sir Richard's face and said, by way of explanation, 'Kaleidoscopic is Pickering Blackburn's system' like any good Lancastrian would.

'I see,' said Sir Richard, not seeing at all, but able to ask the crunch question none the less. 'And had these developments reached a point of commercialization? Profitable commercialization, that is?'

Philip Ashworth smiled faintly. 'That is the hard part,' he murmured. 'There is some question as to whether Pierre —er, Mr Martens—had not reached an impasse along the route he was travelling. One which might need more funds to resolve. He was working very hard on the problem. Indeed, I think he was going at it much too hard. Very often in those circumstances you get so you can't see the wood for the trees. You need to stand back and take it easier. The solution is probably obvious but it won't come when you're so harassed.'

'And was Martens harassed?'

'Very.'

Ashworth's answer came out rather drily. His eyes flicked towards Janssens and then back to his coffee before moving to Sir Richard, then to me. The look he gave me had a significance to it, as though appraising something, then dropped back to his cup.

'So—' Sir Richard wasn't getting what he wanted out of this—'would it be fair to say, in view of this, er, hold-up in Martens' work, that the developments at Rossignol, in your opinion, were not at a stage which would significantly add to the potential value of the company as one would normally assess it?'

He kept himself admirably under control and there was

no impatience in his voice but I knew him of old; he was wearing thin on restraint.

'Oh, I wouldn't say that precisely.' Philip Ashworth put on a serious expression. 'From what we we've been allowed to see to date I think it's possible that the work could be progressed further and perhaps reach a satisfactory conclusion. The logic is quite good, really.'

I stifled a smile. Technical men infuriate commercial ones. It's a different world, where some figures are only estimates and some facts depend on suppositions. You have to use decision theory or some such technique to get any sort of feel for the outcome; pushing at the frontiers of new development is not for the faint of heart. I made up my mind then and there that any price put on Rossignol should, if I were to be asked, discount the development potential entirely. You can lose more money being a pioneer than any black hole could swallow.

'Do you think—' Sir Richard was in remorseless vein now—'that you yourselves at Dillworth's have the ability to complete the work?'

It was an unfair question but Philip Ashworth didn't blink. 'Oh yes,' he said, without expression. 'I'm pretty sure we could cope with it. It's what I've always thought. That's why I've come here.'

Janssens' eyebrows shot up. Sir Richard's jaw dropped, then snapped shut before he spoke. 'You mean—' his voice just managed to stay short of incredulous—'you could simply pick up where Martens left off and put the whole system, whatever it is, into operation?'

Philip Ashworth nodded. 'It'd cost money, of course, but it can be done.'

Janssens frowned. 'Did Pierre Martens tell you enough to make this possible?'

Ashworth smiled. 'Let's just say that the direction of the work is clear to me. What will need to be assessed is the value of what has been done to date and the cost of carrying it to a conclusion.'

'Well.' Sir Richard actually shifted in his chair. 'I must say I'm surprised. But encouraged, of course. It seems as though there may be a really strong argument for this amalgamation. What figures have you in mind?'

Philip Ashworth looked at him, flicked his gaze to me, over to Janssens, took in the blonde beauty of Elizabeth van Laeten, then peered down again.

'I'll have to work that out, Sir Richard,' he murmured. 'Once I've got back to Preston.'

'Not now?'

'Oh no. I need my own systems and computer to do that.' He produced an infuriatingly amiable smile. 'It wouldn't do to give you quick answers on a thing like this, as I'm sure you'll appreciate. It's a very technical matter and it needs time and careful thought.'

'Damn it,' Sir Richard said irritably, losing his rag at last. 'You computer men are all the same, Mr Ashworth. Martens was as cagey when Eugène and I saw him. Never a straight answer where costs were concerned. You're just like him, you know. Very similar. I'm not at all surprised you're inclined to follow on.'

Philip Ashworth's gentle smile faded. His face took on a greyer look, drained and lined, as though going into shock as he peered at Sir Richard and almost whispered his reply.

'Not to the same destination, I hope?'

8

A burnt factory looks just as horrible as a burnt house and the sense of loss is identical. Exposed interiors, streaked and filthy, smudge the eye with their charcoaled relics. Humans once occupied this draughty ruin and, whether they worked or rested in it, safety could be had here. Now, at Wingles, leaves were starting to mingle with the sooty litter. Rain had fallen on the roofless furnishings. Twisted girders or blackened rafters hovered above the remnants. Nothing was secure; all feeling of permanence had gone. The cindered mess threatened any sense of life's meaning or achievement. This, it said, is what can happen, this is what it can come to. No one looks unaffected on the aftermath of a fire.

The concierge in *bleu de travail* walked a part of the way round with me, muttering. I supposed he'd had enough of visitors: police, *pompiers*, fire insurance assessors, forensic men in white disposable overalls, Malfait and his executives, lawyers, magistrate's men, machinery engineers, electricians, even carpet wholesalers, yarn salesmen, chemicals suppliers, and now me, an English banker.

'Did you know Mr Martens well?' I asked casually, more to break the silence than anything. I was waiting for François Kolewski to arrive, having reached the place about ten minutes before the appointed time. Sir Richard had gone back to Paris, leaving me to pursue matters in my own irrational way. One good thing about both Sir Richard and Jeremy White is that they understand that a man doesn't like to be crowded by his superiors while he's trying to think. Or act. In this kind of situation you have to use whatever resources you can bring to hand and Kolewski could well be one of them. At any rate, he'd responded positively enough to my phone call.

'Of course. *Bien sûr.*' The concierge took the question as pure English stupidity. 'Mr Martens worked here for years. A dedicated man. Very clever. The company won't find another like him easily.'

'Mm. Tragic. One wonders how a man like him, so knowledgeable about this business, could have perished in such a fire.'

The concierge gave me a sharp glance. 'It was not so difficult, monsieur. The fire spread like fury.'

'Everyone else got out.'

'*Merci au bon Dieu!* Thank God! They ran like hares. Me too. I thought that Martens was in the office, organizing the exit. The raw material stores, where the fire got going, were down at the far end. You see? Over there. He must have gone to check something he'd forgotten. Or some stock for one of his experiments. He was already late that morning.'

'I beg your pardon?'

'He was late. Unusual for him. Very flustered when he arrived. He worked hard, though, Martens. Always.'

'He had no family, I understand?'

The concierge gave me another rum look. All firms have the same joke: if you want to know what's happening up top, ask the floor sweeper. A concierge will do just as well.

'He was an orphan, yes, monsieur. At least that's what I was told. Some good people in Ghent brought him up— he was Flemish originally but you wouldn't think it; he was a good type. Can't stand *les Flamands* myself. Of course—' the concierge put a finger to his nose—'the orphan tag is often used to conceal the truth, eh?' He winked knowingly as we picked our way over the filthy cinders. 'But Martens spoke well of his foster parents.'

Under the chill damp of a discouraging morning sky we

reached the end of the collapsed wreckage, to a point where the fire had produced its whitest heat. Here there was less black, less sooty coagulate in the grim decoration of the twisted framework. The colours were the grey and ashy white of fire powder. Even some of the upright stanchions had melted, dripping back like candles neglected at a louche dinner table. It seemed hardly credible that steel could run like wax, but there it was.

'This is it,' the concierge said. 'This is the worst part of it. Where Martens must have died.'

The desolation was more intense. What was left here hardly had form at all. Further back there were at least the remains of machinery and identifiable factory areas, dreadful though they seemed, but this looked like the aftermath of an extraordinary explosion which had cleared the space and coated it in chalky dust. Nothing had survived; nothing had retained its shape.

'Ah,' the concierge said, gesturing to break my fascinated concentration, '*voilà Kolewski*.'

Turning, I saw the massive figure of the ex-rugby player from Roubaix heading towards us with a wave, and waved back. If anything, he looked bigger and more dangerous than he had at the meeting in Paris. He was wearing a huge coat of shaggy imitation fur which gave him a really Slavic appearance, more eastern than European, and his broken features, cracked into a smile, produced a grotesque travesty of an amiable greeting.

'Tim! There you are! As punctual as an Englishman!' His smile faded as he looked around. '*Triste, eh?*' He shivered. 'Did you know it was me that gave the alarm?'

I blinked. 'No, I didn't. Didn't see you here when we came. Not at all.'

'I'm not surprised. You came here, according to Janssens, about twenty or thirty minutes after the first big outburst of flame from the stores. By that time I was way round the back and gone to the sheds along the end there to phone Wouvermans—that's my boss at Roubaix, the one you met in Paris—to tell him.' He shook his head sadly and stared at the ruins. '*Triste, triste.*'

'It's more than triste. It's horrible.'

He nodded grimly, then split his face into a cynical expression. 'It's an ill wind, though, Tim. I don't want to shock you, but one has to consider the realities. For the company, I mean. This was an old installation and the stock wasn't moving much either.' He twisted the expression into a significant grimace.

I ran my eyes over his vast shaggy-bear coat and then at the dirty grey powder nearby. 'A rabbit skin, they used to say.'

'Eh?' He gave me a startled look.

'A rabbit skin. An Italian once told me. You soak a rabbit skin in petrol, set it alight and chuck it where the material is inflammable. A rabbit skin leaves no traces or fingerprints.'

A broad, ugly grin came to his face and he nodded. 'I've heard that, too,' he growled. 'Most of the other ways seem to be detectable by the fire investigators.' His ugly grin broadened. 'I can see we've both had some industrial experience since we played rugby together. In fields that don't come in to the training manuals.'

I grinned back. 'Seems like it. Perhaps it says something about the quality of our customers—or employers—or something.'

He nodded ruefully and his eyes rested on my face speculatively for a moment. 'Let's have that beer.'

'Excellent suggestion.'

The concierge stared at us impassively as we thanked him and left, making no comment on the turn our conversation had taken. Kolewski led the way in his car back to the railway level crossing at the central crossroads in Wingles and pulled up outside a bar in a side turning. It

reminded me forcefully yet again of the mill streets in the
north of England; shabby, grimy, damp surroundings unre-
lieved by anything to delight the eye. But the bar was warm
and the plastic upholstery hadn't been slashed, just spot-
burnt through with black-rimmed holes here and there
where smokes and fag-ends had been left smouldering on
it.

Kolewski lit a yellow-papered, black-tobaccoed cigarette,
sucked a thin covering of froth off the top of his golden,
frosty beer and grinned at me over the top of the glass. I
silently toasted him with mine.

'Well, well.' His voice was deep and grainy, sounding as
though it came from somewhere way down inside the
shaggy ursine depths of his massive overcoat. 'Small world,
eh? Do you still play rugby?'

'Nope, not for years.'

'I suppose you're married and got five kids by now?'

I grinned. 'Married, yes. Kids, no. And you?'

He shook his head. 'Not me. Still fancy free.'

'Still playing the field, eh?'

He chuckled. 'That's me; always has been. But I'd never
have guessed you'd become a banker, not all those years
ago. I'd have put you down for industrial or commercial
life, like me.'

'That's the way it goes, François. The cards just fell that
way. You were a terrible man to stop, I remember.'

'You weren't so soft yourself.'

'Playing for Lille, if you didn't go down a mine you were
bound to wind up in the textile industry somewhere.'

'Sure. Worst luck.' He pulled his face into further ugli-
ness. 'I was grateful for the support of the company when
I was playing because it kept the bills paid while I was
away at training or matches. But it's lousy now, Tim, I can
tell you. The textile industry's at the mercy of every little
slant-eyed Chink or Asian bastard in every dirty shed every-

where. Either you fall into the clutches of them or of smooth
shits like Malfait. I'm not sure which is worse.'

My eyes must have widened, for he looked straight into
them and nodded. 'Surprised, are you? What I think of
Malfait? I can tell you, Tim, between you and me only, eh,
we weren't doing too badly until that bastard bought us up
like so many shirts at a market. Martens was working like
stink and promised to achieve something. We were improv-
ing efficiencies all along and there was hope. But the cash
flow wasn't great. So Malfait, that big-time wheeler-dealer,
along with some of his pals at the ministry in Paris and a
certain investment bank behind him—' he rolled his eyes
at me significantly—'did a deal. He snapped us up like
Monopoly property. Sold! He had the Lens place already,
some shares in Roubaix and was sniffing at Vierzon. Every-
body likes Vierzon because it was built on regional development grants, no expense spared, while we struggle along
with old ironwork. Malfait's pals in Paris look at a few
figures on pieces of paper and that's it. Malfait gets the lot
to play his dirty games with. He'll sell us at a profit and
move on when he's lined his pocket well enough. He's no
stayer, I can tell you. We'll be Belgians next. Or English.
Though frankly I think you're wasting your time here. The
English part of the deal won't stick.'

'Oh? Why not?'

His face softened a little. 'The Dillworth Carpet Company? They're too like us. And too far away. If they had
the money they could buy their way on to the Continent,
but an amalgamation doesn't smell right to me. Or we
could buy them, but Malfait won't do that. He'd need too
much more money to prise those Ashworths off their herit-
age—they're not like him, they're the decent old sort that
sticks to its business—and they're too far off, way away
where he can't control things. This is only two hours from
Paris. He'll either go through with Janssens or he'll find

someone else. The industry's not short of sellers. He must be mighty relieved that Martens has snuffed it. It'll save him a lot of money poured into development and I shouldn't wonder if the insurance money won't come in handy. Very convenient, I can tell you. There isn't anyone in the carpet trade who wouldn't rather have cash in hand than old assets in a tufting mill.'

'Jesus.'

'Yes, it makes you think, doesn't it?'

'Have another beer?'

'Thanks.'

I went across to the bar to give myself time to ponder. There are occasions when a past history as a muddied oaf can come in handy. There's not a lot of love lost between English and French rugby players at international level these days, but with the clubs it's different. You can't help making friends from time to time. The only thing that troubled me was that I never remembered being particularly close to Kolewski. The past matches of my Continental tours had all merged into a blur. But who hasn't been back to a school or club reunion and been hailed fervently by someone you never bothered with all those years ago? In later life, scared of passing the moment unrecognized, we tend to embrace people we never looked at then. Recognition from the past reassures us of our present existence. Kolewski was probably delighted to find a face he could claim to know in all the financial upheavals that threatened his work and that of his colleagues. It wasn't unusual.

'Good beer,' I said to him as I sat down, although it was far too cold and gassy for me.

He smiled. 'Surely it should be warm and sour to please you, shouldn't it?'

'Not warm. Cool. And not sour. Bitter.'

He shook his head in mock sadness at this English eccentricity and raised his glass to me. I raised mine back. 'How

long has Malfait been touting for a merger?' I asked, after
I'd downed a suitable draught.

He swallowed, then took a pull on his reeking cigarette.
'Almost from the day he bought it.' Smoke billowed from
him. 'There was a big address to the employees, promises
of big investment to ensure future jobs, blah, blah, blah,
the usual crap, then in no time we heard of the "exploratory
talks" between Rossignol and Louis Janssens. To secure
the future of the company in these difficult times, blah,
blah, blah. More of the usual crap.'

'Then the Dillworth dimension came in.'

'Precisely. The Dillworth dimension. To muddy the
waters. A red herring, Tim, with no disrespect to your
courtly Sir Richard. An English gentleman of the old
school. Malfait will drag the Dillworth red herring about
to make sure he gets the right terms.' He put a smoking
finger to his nose. 'Make no mistake: Malfait is a tough
baby. He plays for big game. With big artillery.'

'And the computer aspect?'

'*Merde* to the computer aspect! So Martens is dead. Malfait is nothing if not a realist. He knows he can't progress
much further right now without Martens, but there are
assistants, people who can keep things turning over. He
could even get a new man from outside. No one is entirely
indispensable, Tim, not even you and me. Malfait will be
quite prepared to put up a smoke screen or buy the technology from somewhere else. It can be done. If—' he held up
a finger—'if Malfait wants to carry on. Who knows? Even
that Philip Ashworth might find the answer and sell it. Or
some Jap, or a Swiss. But not until they've done a hell of a
lot of work.'

'I must say I worried about how much was being re-
vealed before the deal was fully signed, sealed and de-
livered.'

Kolewski shrugged. 'To my knowledge only the principal

direction of the research was indicated. It's the detail that's valuable and that's safely locked away. All those thousands of hours of trial and error; they are what cost the money, Tim.'

'Of course. But it'll be difficult to demonstrate anything now. Tell me: how well did you know Martens?'

He scowled. 'Martens? He was a Wingles man. I'm from Roubaix. I mean, we worked for different companies originally, so the back history doesn't go far. But after Malfait put us together Martens came up to Roubaix to test some parts of his process on our equipment. Wouvermans made me the liaison man, so I got to know Martens a bit. A cagey fellow. Belgian, you know, Flemish. Not terribly communicative. I'll tell you something, though: he and that chap Ashworth, Philip Ashworth, they got on well. Similar men, very similar; computer freaks.'

I smiled. 'That's what Sir Richard said.'

'Well, he's right. They spoke the same language, you could see that. Fortran, or some other computer lingo.'

I grinned. 'Did Martens have any particular friends? He had no family, it seems.'

Kolewski shook his head. 'Not that I know of. He lived in Lens. Kept himself to himself. An orphan type.'

'No girlfriends?'

'Not that I know of.' Kolewski frowned. 'No. You have to realize that I only worked with him and I'm not a computer man. He didn't confide in me personally.'

'The concierge said that his foster parents were in Ghent.'

'Oh? Yes, I believe he once mentioned that. But it's nothing to me.'

'You said that the detail of his work is safe. You mean it didn't go up in smoke here at Wingles?'

'One set did. We have a duplicate—floppy discs, systems designs, the works—at Roubaix. There's another set with Malfait in Paris.'

'Well, that's a relief. Someone had foresight.'

He shrugged. 'Standard security practice.' Then he narrowed his eyes at me. 'Martens did show your crowd some of the process here. But that Eugène Maucourt from your Paris Bank is a cold fish.'

'You bet.'

'I've only met him twice, once in Roubaix and once here with Martens because I'm the Roubaix liaison man; that's why I was here the day of the fire. I can't see that it'd be easy to make friends with Eugène Maucourt.'

'It isn't, François, let me tell you. He and I do not belong to the same clubs, that's for sure.'

He nodded slowly. 'So it looks as though Maucourt will fight Malfait's case with everything he's got.'

'Absolutely. That's what Malfait retains Maucourt Frères for.'

Kolewski nodded slowly and looked at his empty glass. 'In that case, Tim, how about another beer? It looks as though, for us at Roubaix, you might be the best hope.'

I glanced outside. A thin rain had started to fall again, blown by a cold gusty breeze of the sort we'd had at Cuinchy that first fateful morning. It spattered and dampened the hard buildings with a shiny film of dirty moisture that somehow heightened the presence of grime and the broken state of the pavement opposite. The bar was warm and the beer was just starting to release fingers of soporific ease along my arms and legs. I began to feel comfortably grubby as my mind kept flinching from that white-ashed hollow where the holocaust had consumed Pierre Martens.

'Another beer, why not?' I said. 'For absent friends.'

Kolewski grinned his savage grin. 'Absent friends,' he rumbled, and trundled off to the bar in his great shaggy coat, trailing malodorous ash in the way that only the Continentals seem to do nowadays.

I suppose Sir Richard would have something to say about prejudice at that observation.

9

Busloads of schoolchildren milled round the entrance to the
Hayward Gallery, cluttering the access and giggling at one
of Toulouse-Lautrec's can-can girls postered with her leg
cocked high in the air. I managed to get through without
pushing anyone or making rude remarks about that concrete bunker of a building, perched between the wrong end
of Waterloo Bridge and the Festival Hall like a blockhouse
set in enemy territory, even though it cost the same five
pounds to get in, whether you wanted to see the Toulouse-
Lautrec or the Contemporary Art Society's travelling exhibition or both; there was no point in demanding a discount.

Getting back to London was a relief. It gave me a sense
of distance and objectivity. The Continent was safely tucked
away, as it were, somewhere across the Channel where it
couldn't get at me. Or at least it felt as though it couldn't.
There was an intensity of depression about that area around
Lille, with its run-down industries, its local passions and
past horrors, that I needed to avoid for a bit. Call it escap-
ism and you'd be right. I was having one of my chicken
periods, not to mention a hangover from my session with
Kolewski.

Sue had been delighted to see me back. I gave her a brief
rundown on what I was doing, without any emphasis on
the rather sinister aspects, just keeping to the problems of
the merger, and she listened as dutifully as should a wife.
On the whole, the women I know find industry extremely
boring and I can't say I blame them; it's far more interesting to look at the finished goods in the shops than to go
through the whole palaver of how they got there.

The CAS material was upstairs at the Hayward, safely

above Lautrec's low records of caperings, vice, brothel queens and crusty lechers. I got to it in a succession of strides up the reversing grey staircase and paused for breath as the full impact hit me. They were all there, with artists from the Art Fund's somewhat violent past and their contemporaries, like Augustus John and his sister Gwen, mingling with Sickert, Gertler, Wilson Steer, Henry Lamb, Duncan Grant, Wyndham Lewis in vorticist angularity, and, appropriately next to him, almost firing straight at his geometrical Praxitella, the agonized machine-gun post of Nevinson's graphic experience and imagination in all its grey-blue, metallic tones.

La Mitrailleuse.

Usually, I curse like mad when the Tate lends out its paintings. It means you can't find the bloody things or you have to traipse off to somewhere like Liverpool to look at them. The paintings that aren't on view or on loan are parked in the Tate's basement and you can get to see those by making an appointment but I didn't want to make an appointment: I didn't want to bump into Sue or have one of her friends tell her I was lurking about the place on a clandestine assignation, playing truant from work. If I want to see a painting in the Tate's basement I get Sue to show it to me but Sue not unnaturally wants to hear the full chapter and verse, what the hell it's all about, what mischief the Art Fund is getting me into next. Since I wasn't buying a Nevinson and the whole business of Ashworth's Nevinson was peripheral to what I was doing, I didn't want to start a strong muscular hare running like mad in Sue's mind about some mayhem or other connected with art.

My mistake, of course.

I did want to see the painting, which was out on loan with the CAS exhibition at the Hayward Gallery before going off on tour, to Liverpool among other places. There was a limited chance to view. It was just curiosity really, just a sort of mental thirst, a feeling that Nevinson was someone I knew a little about but not really enough. When an artist crosses your path like that, and you're buzzing around the area of France where his war work got its vivid inspiration, you get these nagging desires to complete the dossier, settle the mind, in much the same way as Janssens had perhaps had when researching Graves and wanting to get a view of where it all happened, what it looked like. I could sympathize with that.

La Mitrailleuse isn't a big painting. It's about twenty-four inches by twenty—I should say 60 cm by 50 cm now we've gone all metric—and it's framed in a bronzed moulding that's not too wide. The image is almost a cliché now: a helmeted French machine-gunner, bearded and desperate, hemmed in by sharp trench carpentry and wire, eyes masked, stares along the square grey casing of his horrid equipment at a dreaded invisible foe. Below his red trousers the bleached countenance of a dead companion looks sightlessly upwards: another sightless live face under a helmet shouts urgently: a third companion crouches to stare fearfully in the direction of the gun. The streaked sky, hardly visible above the spiky dugout, is tangled with wire. The sharp edges of this jagged world are echoed in the angled features of the Cubist faces and clothes. Nothing is soft or rounded; the images could be those of men trapped in a submarine's engine-room just before the explosion of a fatal depth charge outside.

It is hard to believe now that due to what had been a haze of patriotic war fever and media glorification the painting caused a sensation when it was exhibited in 1916. People seeing it and the terrible wounded men of *La Patrie* realized that this, not what they read in the papers, was what things were really like. Sickert said that *La Mitrailleuse* was the most authoritative and concentrated utterance on the war yet made. Even the Bloomsburies were impressed. Nevinson was a controversial figure but a humane man; his work as a Red Cross ambulance driver had given him a wider view of the war than many soldiers had seen. He was just twenty-seven and he believed he was on the threshold of a great career.

How many of us, I wondered as I stared at the machine-gunner's grim angles, believe that the future is all there, up for grabs, when in reality the best is over and done with? Ironically the young Nevinson once saw Toulouse-Lautrec in the flesh, rather drunk at his London exhibition; yet again they were under the same roof.

'Tim!'

The voice made me jump about a foot in the air. Sue's tones are unmistakable.

'It is! It is you!'

Shock transfixed me; this couldn't be happening. I froze solid in front of the painting.

'Tim?' The tones were incredulous. 'What on earth are you doing here?'

Just when you think you have everything all worked out, Fate's boomerang hits you right in the back of the neck.

I smiled weakly as I turned stiffly. 'Oh, er, hello, Sue.'

She stood in front of me, coat loosely slung, bag in hand, posture rigid. Her eyes were, to put it mildly, wide open. Her expression was not yet alarmed but it wasn't very reassured, either. Nervously strung curiosity radiated out like static, I'd have said. Rather intently focused. On me.

'Why in heaven's name aren't you at work? And why are you here, goggling at that awful war picture of Nevinson's? What's going on?'

'I—um—I saw the exhibition was on and I, er, well, I nipped in. More to see the Toulouse-Lautrecs than any-thing, I suppose. A passing whim, you might say. Just wandered up here. I was going to tell you, of course.'

She drew herself up. Her eyes narrowed. Other visitors

had somehow deserted us and it seemed as though we were entirely alone, surrounded by canvases. Sue's speciality is the Impressionists. The CAS have had a close relationship with the Tate Gallery since the beginning. It was, I now realized, a stone cold racing certainty that she'd be in here at least once, and just when I thought she'd be safely immured in her basement office at the Tate, here she was.

'Just passing? You never go past the Hayward. You're fibbing. You're going as red as a beetroot. Guilt in every line of your face. Tim, what on earth are you up to?'

I got a grip of myself and responded bravely. 'I am not guilty. Not at all. I'm just viewing the exhibition. Come to that, what are you doing here? You know all these pictures well enough, including those brothel queens downstairs.' I gestured at a Burra to indicate another brothel queen. 'All in your range. I'm not nearly as familiar with them as you are. Why are you here?'

'You're supposed to be dealing in carpets.' She ignored all my questions. 'You've never mentioned going to the Hayward once. You don't even like Toulouse-Lautrec.' She grimaced at *La Mitrailleuse*. 'Nevinson? Nevinson? For God's sake, Tim, if the Art Fund is going to buy a Nevinson, why didn't you tell me instead of sneaking a peek at one like this? Why haven't you mentioned it?'

'I am not sneaking a peek! Besides—' I waved round grandly—'all my old friends are represented here.'

'That's what worries me.' Anxiety was flooding into her voice. 'I've come over for a quiet look at the exhibition and the way it's all been hung and I find you prowling about among a back history of mayhem, staring at that machine-gun.' She shivered. 'That painting has always given me the creeps.'

'It's meant to give you the creeps.' My eye went back to the dark menace of the canvas. 'It's the weapon that destroyed millions. A piece of symbolism of the highest order.'

'Really, Tim! I do not need a lecture on Nevinson, or on machine-guns. What I want to know is what you're doing here. And why you haven't asked me.'

I licked my lips. It was perfectly fair, of course. What I was doing to her was the equivalent of Sue taking up investment banking without telling me. The trouble was that I hadn't wanted to disturb her. And this was where my consideration had got me.

So I took her arm and steered her, protesting, into the coffee shop, then sat her down and told her. Carefully, calmly, keeping to the major facts, not playing anything particularly up or down, just as it had all happened to date. Event by event, watching her close her eyes in mock despair, open them, close them, then open them again, especially when I confessed that I'd been about to consult her when I got back from Darwen but other events had intervened. She finished her coffee, put her hand on mine and shook her head in mock sadness.

'You just can't keep out of it, can you?'

'What?'

'Trouble, of course. I know.' She held up a hand to stop me from speaking. 'You'll say it's all Jeremy's, or this time Sir Richard's, fault but you know you love it. That's why they use you. You love it and you're good at it.' She twinkled at me as she held up a cautionary finger. 'And I know you're just trying not to upset me by keeping me in the dark. But you mustn't. Have I helped you in the past or haven't I?'

'You've helped me. More than somewhat.'

'Do you want me to help you now? With the Nevinson, of course, not anything else. I'm not going over to that awful batch of carpet factories to fight fires and argue with evil industrialists.'

Her eyebrows arched at me. Irresistibly.

'Of course I want you to help me.'

'You are such an idiot, Tim. You know I always find out, but you always do this.'

'I know. I'm sorry. People never change, you see.'

'I'm not sure about that. Let's go and have a look.'

She got up, took my hand, dead pleased with herself, and led me back into the gallery like a child being walked round by its mother. I went along obediently; I know when not to push my luck.

At the spot where she'd discovered me she stopped to stare yet again at the grim concentration of Nevinson's stylized machine-gunner, masked by helmet and beard, gazing fearfully at an unseen, oncoming, unrelenting menace.

'Tell me,' she asked after a while, with that maddening, simplistic perception an uninformed outsider often brings to a complex problem, 'where do the Germans fit into all this?'

10

The preliminary gin and tonics had been doubles. The Meursault had gone down well with the soup and fish. The Château Clarke 1986 Listrac, Rothschild—a modest claret in the circumstances but one of which I was getting very fond—was not yet by any means completely finished, even though the prime steak was. The cloth was relatively clear in preparation for the sweet trolley, or the Stilton, or both. Vintage port could be secured from the offing without delay or demur. The afternoon stretched ahead in a potentially joyous haze of good conversation and cheerful repartee.

'Well, well.' Jeremy White was at his most genial. 'This is a turn-up for the old book, I must say. For your European budget to be able to stand me a decent lunch for a change is a real reversal of roles. Not that I'm in any way complaining, I'm sure. It had never occurred to me that, after all those years of lunching you, Tim, you'd be able to turn the tables on me. Turn the tables, ha-ha, get the joke? No? Well, never mind. If Uncle Richard's little capers across the Continent bring me a half-reasonable lunch of the old sort once in a while I shan't perhaps cavil at your absence quite so miserably as I might otherwise do.' He sighed heavily. 'It really has become quite a dismal business, working in the City these days, Tim. Nothing to what it was. People sipping filthy bottled waters full of sulphur or poisonous minerals and crumbling a dry biscuit. Nobody seems to eat a decent meal any more, let alone drink a noggin or two. They all claim to be at their desks at seven, or some such inconceivable hour, and to be mad on PT, or gym, or whatever they call it now. It's the American influence, you know. We should have nothing to do with it.'

'I'm sure you're right, Jeremy.'

'I know I'm right. Life is for living, Tim. You're a long time dead, dear boy.' His face brightened again. 'What an excellent idea of yours this was. D'you remember those super lunches, in the dear departed days of Park Lane, when business was business and lunch was lunch?'

'Never forgotten them.'

'By Heaven, there's twenty better restaurants up in the West End for every one in this dreary neck of the woods. And business was fun, then. Real fun, not all this long-faced drudgery. We turned a doubloon or two in those days, didn't we?'

'It was a very profitable activity, Jeremy.'

'It certainly was. Left this crowd standing. Even Geoffrey, who is an accountant before he is a human being, was quite cheerful in those days. Cautious, of course. Always cautious, our Geoffrey. He sent you his best, by the way.'

'Oh? Not gone away, has he?'

'What?' For a moment Jeremy looked startled. 'No, no, of course not. He's only briefly off on business somewhere. But he says he sees little of you now. Says you're always *chez les Maucourts* and so on. Wanted to know how you were.'

'Return my compliments. Tell him I'll see him all too soon.'

'Really? Oh well, of course. I'll do that.' He nodded affably as the waiter filled his glass and mine with the last of the Château Clarke, and turned a rosy countenance on me with a cheerful grin. 'Geoffrey, it has to be said, has taken to the City like an embalmer to an undertaker's emporium.'

I chuckled. 'Really?'

'How he loves the doom and gloom! How he wallows in the post-Big Bang massacres! There's nothing like an announcement of big broker redundancies to bring a smile to Geoffrey's lips. "I told you so" is a phrase he repeats so often I've threatened to record it and play it back to him every ten minutes. Accountancy with a capital A, that's our Geoffrey, eh?'

'Always was.'

'How right you are, Tim.'

'It was a good thing sometimes, mark you.'

'Sometimes, Tim, sometimes, but not often. Look at the paintings we acquired for the Art Fund while he wrung his hands and wailed. Superb things. At what are still marvellous prices. I don't share this post-Maxwell condemnation of all entrepreneurial activities, you know. Not at all. Nothing venture, nothing gain. There's a limit to all things, I have to agree, but one simply can't have all this, er, this accountability and paperwork and auditors with their sticky little quill pens in everything. No scope that way. No scope at all.'

'Perhaps not, Jeremy.'

'Talking of paintings, you haven't had your gimlet eye on anything lately, have you?'

I shook my head. 'I can't really say that I have, Jeremy.'

He gave me a suspicious squint. 'No, as a matter of fact, I can't detect that beady look you acquire when you're up to mischief on the art side. Furtive, you get. My goodness, life really has got a bit dim, hasn't it, Tim, when you haven't got a prospect in view and Geoffrey's chuckling over the obituary notices in the Company News?'

'Things are a bit grey at present, Jeremy.'

'Got plenty of cash in hand, haven't we?'

'Oh yes. The Art Fund is pretty liquid. But there's not much about that I'd want to have a go at. The better stuff is holding back until things pick up.'

'Ah, Tim! In how many fields do I hear that wimpish wail? "Until things pick up." Things will never pick up, dear boy, unless people like us take the initiative! Have a go! Untrammel yourself from this madness of Uncle

Richard's and get back on the trail! Find us a splendid painting or some art treasure or another! Much better to spend your time on that than skulking under the Belgian cotton or whatever, I'm sure.'

I just refrained from pointing out that it had not been more than a few days since he'd made his nasty remarks about my tendencies vis-à-vis art mayhem and waited patiently while he was served with a basinful of profiteroles and cream from the sweet trolley.

'Talking of Belgian cotton—' I waved the same trolley away with a regretful gesture—'you didn't by any chance get in touch with Philip Ashworth after all, did you?'

'Mmm?' Mouth full of chocolate, cream and pastry, he frowned at me.

'Philip Ashworth. In touch?'

He shook his head carefully. 'No,' he mumbled, 'I didn't contact him.'

Jeremy is very scrupulous about technical truthfulness. I leant forward as he finished his calorific mouthful.

'He contacted you then, didn't he? Some time ago? About Germany, perhaps?'

He swallowed. His pressured eye went back down wistfully to the rest of the profiteroles in front of him. Thoughts were obviously racing through his brain. I kept my head forward.

'Let me make it a bit easier for you, Jeremy. You've been following the BCD affair closely. The Ashworths are a cunning crowd. They've got more sense than to put all their eggs in one basket and I'm certain they don't trust the French or the Belgians. The Germans have a huge market and many of the major machinery makers. Up to now they've been using East Germany as a cheap extra source of production but unification is going to change the cost of all that. Their other cheap source was Yugoslavia—they didn't recognize Croatia before anyone else out of pure altruism—but the Croats and Serbs are doing their best to murder each other while destroying the economy and business generally. So it might make sense to look elsewhere. Like Lancashire, for instance.'

He muttered something indistinguishable and put down his spoon, then took hold of it again.

'What is more—' I watched him fiddle another profiterole back on to the spoon—'the Germans have concentrated on new technology and Philip Ashworth is no slouch at that. So, while his uncle is drawing the French and Belgians' fire around Lille, it wouldn't be inconceivable that he and you met to work out a German approach on the side, would it?'

He got his breath back. 'Really, Tim, you have no—'

'After all, you're both nephews together, aren't you? It must be quite fun for each of you watching old uncle getting singed around Wingles while you two youngsters do the business over the border with the Krauts.'

'Tim!'

'Except that Philip Ashworth and his uncle are like two peas in a pod. You and Sir Richard, on the other hand, are too busy worsting each other to appreciate that.'

'Enough! Enough! To think that I was enjoying this lunch! You creature!'

'Do you deny that you are collaborating with Philip Ashworth to examine a German alternative to the BCD affair?'

'I certainly do! The measures I take for my clients are in entire confidence. You are in the Maucourts' pocket, you and Richard together. There's a conflict of interest with Malfait here.'

I smiled in relief. 'So you admit you're working for Philip. Who, by the way, is looking rather pale and wan. Not at all the yachtsman I was led to believe in. It must be crouching over computers that does it. Are you still denying the German part, too?'

'Yes, I am, damn it! I—er—I have shown a friendly
interest out of an old friendship with Philip. It would be
churlish not to discuss matters with him. The Ashworths
are important clients. You're jumping to conclusions. I cannot think what gave you the idea that there was any German
involvement from my side. Why should the subject of Germany come into it at all?'

I smiled even wider. I know my Jeremy and I moved in
with pleasure to deliver the *coup de grâce*, while refraining
from reminding him of his previous remarks about imposing
commercialism upon old acquaintance.

'It was Sue who suggested it, as a matter of fact. With
one of her brilliant shafts of perception. But in any case,
Jeremy, I think you should know that Geoffrey, our dear
friend and accountant with a capital A, who reports directly
to you in every particular, arrived in Frankfurt on time.
There's fax on the machine to say so. It comes from Hartmann Tufting AG, who say he'll be back tomorrow as
planned. After their discussions.'

A piece of profiterole cascaded on to his silk tie. His face
went quite mottled. 'You—you—read my fax? My private
fax?'

'It just happened to be on the Bank's machine as I was
passing. But to be absolutely honest it was you who put the
notion into my head. Sue's question only reminded me. You
see, when I came back from France the last time you rather
ironically called me a *Wunderkind*, which is German for
whizzkid. I've never heard you use the word before. It's
funny how dealing with people makes you drop into their
vernacular.' I gave him an encouraging beam as he mopped
congestedly at his tie. ''Appen as 'ow I'm finding that
meself, an' all. Or summat.'

11

The Preston mill of the Dillworth Carpet Company was more imposing than the Darwen one and most of it seemed to have been built later. It certainly looked a bit newer. It was outside the town on a rather bleak eastern-facing bank of the River Ribble exposed to withering winds when they were in the wrong direction, but sheltered, I supposed, most of the time from the prevailing south-westerlies which supply the area with generous amounts of rain. There were two high brick chimneystacks to dominate both the buildings and the car park but I realized, as I got out of the car into the driving downpour, that neither of them was smoking. Like most of Lancashire's remaining mill chimneys, they were totems of a past industrial civilization, more for worship than for use.

The foyer of the offices vibrated gently with the encouraging hum of distant machinery. A receptionist in a green nylon work coat with 'Dillworth' printed in red on its top pocket sent for Philip Ashworth's secretary, who was suitably young, as befitted the image of an R & D department, rather than the comfortable middle age of Jack Ashworth's Darwen Doris. This secretary tripped along the corridors ahead of me chatting amiably of the latest pile-up on the M6, one which I had queued patiently to pass on my way up from Manchester Airport. They enjoy news of a good car smash in those parts; it makes them feel that life is a bit riskier than the daily grind suggests.

Philip Ashworth greeted me cautiously. He was wearing a long white coat and his office was untidily piled with carpet samples of every description, giving the feeling that he only perched in his office between forays to the production line. On his large desk, however, was a PC of the latest type with a baffling extra modem covered in abstruse keyboards and visual sub-displays. Printouts and charts were piled high around it. This was clearly the office of a technical man much given to computer analysis.

He waved me to a chair and returned to his on the other side of the desk, peering at me guardedly across the barricade of computer equipment, paper, and bits of carpet.

'I hear there's been another bad smash on the M6,' he said, keeping his opening gambit cheerfully topical. 'I'm glad to see you must have missed it.'

'Oh yes. Just south of town but above the M61 junction. I saw the aftermath. Not very nice.'

'No, these things never are.'

'A bit like going to Wingles, really.'

He flinched. 'Oh dear,' he murmured.

His face pulled into a pained expression. There was no doubt that he was an Ashworth, as I've said, but he had none of his Uncle Jack's robust ebullience. He was smaller, thinner, much more cautious, if Jack Ashworth had any caution at all. Yet the sense of resolution remained; this was not a weak man. I wondered which part of the war-torn Ashworth family had brought him up; obviously not Jack Ashworth's side, despite his avuncular pride in his nephew.

'Did you know Martens well?'

Philip Ashworth licked his lips. 'Well? Er, no, not really. I mean, there wasn't time. We've only been looking at this proposed collaboration for a short time, you know.'

'Sure. But you and he were rather key to much of the assessment of things. Along with Janssens' computer people, of course.'

'Janssens?' He suddenly looked sharp, then his expression faded. 'Oh, Louis Janssens as a firm. Of course. Bob Janssens himself isn't a computer man.'

'No. But what was the feeling of his people when you saw them, just before we met?'

He stroked his jaw. 'It was odd, really.'

'Odd?'

'Yes. Very odd. I mean, I wasn't too impressed by them. I didn't think they'd got much to offer. But the other day I got the impression that they didn't care very much. About Pierre—er, Martens'—work, I mean.'

'Didn't care?'

'No. As though it didn't matter.'

I frowned. Kolewski had been rather dismissive of the effect of Martens' death, too. As though Malfait might almost be relieved of the financial burden of such work. 'The whole merger is affected, surely, by the computer aspects? I mean, the arguments for combining, faced with firms like Beaulieu Tufting in Belgium, are already well known, but the computer development work was supposed to be a very valuable additional incentive.'

'I know.'

Like Sir Richard, I was beginning to find his reticence a bit frustrating. 'Look, Philip—I hope you don't mind my calling you Philip?'

'Not at all.'

'Well, this business has some strange and sinister aspects, Philip. Do you know that?'

His answering look sharpened again. 'Sinister?'

'Yes, sinister. Martens phoned Sir Richard White shortly before the proposed meeting at Wingles to say that he believed he was in danger. He wanted a private meeting.'

'Good heavens.'

'He never mentioned anything to you?'

'Not—not in so many words, no.'

'Look, I know you got on well with him because everyone in France says so. Did he confide in you at all? Anything, almost anything you can remember, might be important.'

Philip Ashworth hesitated, then spoke slowly. 'There was a good deal in common between us, yes. I must say I liked him. I understood the drift of his work completely. That's why I said at Janssens' place that I'm sure it could be completed although I haven't worked out the cost yet. I could follow his logic. His block on the bit where he'd got stuck just needed systematic work, that's all. He was worried about it, though. He worked long hours on it. He seemed very preoccupied, not so much the first time I met him as afterwards. He didn't reveal any more information than he should but we were on very friendly terms. We had lunch and dinner together.'

'Dinner? Where, in Lens?'

'Yes.' Philip Ashworth gave me a curious stare. 'How did you know that?'

'Because he lived there. Did he tell you much about himself?'

Ashworth frowned. Now he seemed to choose his words carefully. 'Only that he didn't have a family. Why, what importance does that have?'

'I don't know. He was late in to work that morning— the morning of the fire—and I wondered whether the delay was from work or personal.'

'My guess would be work.'

'I'm surprised that you didn't come to the meeting at Wingles since it was, after all, to do with Martens' work. I suppose you were in Germany that day?'

His eyes shot open. He stared at me almost like a man in shock. But he didn't speak, so I didn't stop.

'The discussions with Hartmann Tufting would need a technical man. Their outfit is said to be quite advanced. Your Uncle Jack would be OK for Wingles because he probably wanted to satisfy himself and you'd already covered most of what we would see.'

Philip Ashworth didn't speak. He just stared at me.

'I think, Philip, I should tell you that I occupy a position in the No-Man's-Land between the *mitrailleuse* of Sir Richard and Maucourt Frères on the one hand and Jeremy's bren gun on the other. So you see I'm trying to hold a balance between them, which requires an agility I may not have. But I have told Jeremy I know about your approaches to Hartmann Tufting and I won't let on to Malfait via Maucourt's. You have my assurance on that. Ashworth's are clients and we guarantee confidentiality.'

For the first time he smiled slightly. 'You must be in quite a difficult position,' he said. 'I've known all about Jeremy and his Uncle Richard since our days at Oxford together.'

'It's not easy. But it keeps life interesting.'

His smile widened. 'Jeremy says you've done brilliant things with his Art Fund.'

'We've had a good run so far.'

The smile faded. 'I wish,' he said, coming up with it straight out of the blue, 'I wish you'd buy that bloody Nevinson painting off Uncle Jack.'

It was my turn to blink. With one bound we had left the complexities of the BCD and jumped straight into the Art Fund and all my suspicions. 'Why? Why on earth do you want me to do that?'

'Because—' his face was clouded and anxiety came into his voice—'it's bloody unlucky for our family and Jack should never have hung it up.' He leant earnestly across the broad expanse of his desk. 'I want it out before something terrible happens to yet another one of us.'

12

As we assembled in the gracious meeting-room off the Rue du Faubourg Saint-Honoré, Eugène Maucourt took his place at the head of the table. His glacial eye took in the persons present and made the slightest of expressional changes to indicate that he had seen me. Towards Sir Richard he extended the change of expression so as to spread it to a warmer cast of countenance. It has to be said that the whole reason for the connection with Maucourt Frères came, on the part of White's Bank, from Sir Richard having been involved, during the Second World War, in the Resistance with Eugène's father, Charles Maucourt. He and the splendid old boy were close friends. Eugène, on the other hand, demonstrated a Gaullist frostiness towards *les Anglo-Saxons* which would have done credit to Ice-Cold Couve de Murville, or any other Gaullist right back up to The General himself. Add to this basic attitude my having turned down a job in Paris he once offered me and a general distrust of my presence on his territory, in much the same way as British troops have always been distrusted by many French regulars or irregulars, and you have the essential ingredients for the reason why he and I never exactly embrace each other. To Sir Richard, on the other hand, he has to extend some warmth due to the latter's friendship with his father, his Francophilia, house in the Dordogne, excellent French, his Croix de Guerre medal for services in the Franche-Comté during the last bit of bother and, last but far from least, his presence on the board of directors of Maucourt Frères as part of the cross-ownership of shares worked out when the two banks got together.

On the other hand Jean Malfait, seated on Eugène

Maucourt's right, betrayed no coolness in his glossy exterior. He nodded almost affably in my direction. His suit shone with the shine of expensive fibres winnowed from the coats of rare animals. His white hair, abundant and wavy, was neatly controlled in combed splendour, sweeping back from his pink forehead in expensively-groomed and carefully-considered shaping. His aroma was of costly after-shave or cologne. I noticed, before he sat down, that his shoes were handmade Italian and fitted his feet perfectly, without losing a millimetre of style. The sight of him made me think of François Kolewski, shaggy and ash-scattered, sitting craggily in a cheap bar in seedy Wingles, worrying about the fate of the Roubaix factory.

Yet here we were, about to put the last touches to the proposed mergers. Men like Kolewski and Wouvermans, and all those under them, had their fates decided at meetings like this. Perhaps that was why Malfait exuded bonhomie: he was in sight of an objective.

Bob Janssens was wearing yet another suit. This one was dark, with a faint stripe, and a dark tie, set against a cream shirt, matched it. He still looked fit and tanned, so tanned that I wondered whether he was perpetuating his holiday brown by the use of a sun-lamp. He also looked fresh and well; whatever the combined strains of maintaining family life and enjoying the delights of the radiant Elizabeth van Laeten might be imposing, they weren't wearing him down. On the table in front of him he placed a thin leather document case, a soft thing with a zip round it and his initials monogrammed in gold in one corner, and took a few papers out of it.

Sir Richard White sat next to me, but higher up the table, nearer the top. On the other side sat Jacques Charville, facing me in a suitably below-the-salt situation. He had given me a rather feverish greeting as we came in and handed me a thick dossier, at which I had only glanced before closing it again quickly, mainly because it was chock full of stultifying statistics.

There was a slight sense of tension in the air, even though this was supposed to be a fairly straightforward review meeting, with Janssens present to endorse or discuss whatever steps came next on behalf of Louis Janssens, and Sir Richard to monitor on behalf of Dillworth's. The whole thing was reaching crunch point. Despite the fire, Malfait had called for this meeting to determine the last principles before lawyers were let loose on the details so as to make their fortunes.

The business started with Eugène intoning one of his notorious *tours d'horizon*, summarizing the major values and figures put into the proposed deal, with poor Charville nodding excitedly from time to time so as to provide encouragement. We all waited politely enough for it to finish and then, like greyhounds let off the leash, Malfait and Janssens shot off simultaneously after the rabbit.

'Excellent—' Malfait, pompously grand.

'Dreadful—' Janssens, tensely sharp.

They both stopped. Malfait stared at Janssens in haughty dignity, as a Frenchman might look at a Fleming who'd interrupted him.

'Pardon?' he demanded.

'I said dreadful. A complete travesty.' Janssens was emphatic.

Sir Richard shot me an alarmed glance. Charville bit his lip.

'Travesty? What do you mean?'

Janssens' face, I now noticed, had a stubborn rigidity under its tan. He spoke tightly, directing his gaze accusingly at Malfait and Eugène Maucourt. 'This whole proposal is a complete travesty. A catalogue of misinformation. We have been completely misled.'

'Misled?' Even Eugène Maucourt's icy calm had gone. 'What do you mean?'

'I mean—' Janssens waved a hand at the papers which had come out of the monogrammed case—'that I have here the calculations of my experts on the value of the Rossignol enterprise. They come to about half of what has been put into the summaries of Rossignol and Maucourt Frères. It is one of the most blatant and unprofessional attempts to overvalue a company that I have ever seen.'

He then sat back and glared at everyone. Except me; he seemed to avoid looking at me.

Utter silence ensued for a moment. Then everyone except me starting talking at once.

'Incredible—' Malfait

'Take great exception—' Eugène Maucourt

'For Heaven's sake, Bob—' Sir Richard

'But, but, but—' Jacques Charville

Very noisy, it was. I had a feeling that Jack Ashworth would have enjoyed it immensely. For about thirty seconds there was a complete babble, then Malfait's voice, deep bass, surmounted all.

'Explain yourself!' he shouted at Janssens.

'Certainly!' The reply, higher pitched, stopped the other voices. Janssens glared at Malfait again. 'We have been misled on the efficiency, productivity and condition of the Rossignol factories. Only Vierzon meets any kind of modern standard. We have been misled also on the work of poor Martens, to whom I bear no ill-will, but who was completely stuck in his line of development.'

'Stuck?' Malfait's colour had gone from pink to deep red. 'What in hell do you mean, stuck?'

'I mean that there is no value to be put on his work. It cannot be assessed in any form of value for the purpose of our discussions.'

'Of course it can! It is highly valuable! We have evidence, we are confident!'

'In that case I congratulate you. I advise you to continue. But as far as Louis Janssens is concerned, the value for Rossignol we accept is—' Bob Janssens groped among his papers—'this one.'

He rapped out a figure. Malfait's face turned from deep red to purple.

'What?' he shouted.

Janssens repeated the figure.

Malfait rose, towering, from his chair. 'This is an insult! A dereliction of an agreed and fully-intended agreement discussed and entered into in good faith!'

'A deception!' Janssens retorted. 'A deliberate attempt at deceit!'

'My God! Eugène! Follow me!'

Malfait swept out, followed by a stunned Eugène Maucourt. Janssens stared round for a moment, grimaced, stuffed his papers into his case, and stood up.

'Bob—' Sir Richard was on his feet as well. 'Bob, please—'

'No!' Janssens glared at him. 'I'm sure your role has had honest intentions. But when you speak to those two cheats you can tell them my figure is final! If that chiseller Malfait wants to unload Rossignol, he's heard my price. Not a cent more. And don't bring Maucourt near me again. He's not welcome.'

With that he too swept out. Sir Richard stared after him, looked at me, stared again, then left the room in the direction of Eugène's office.

'Stay there!' he shouted, over his shoulder. 'Wait for me!'

I had been about to get up but I did as I was told and stayed in my chair. A sudden irreverent thought speculated what all of them might have said if they had found out about Hartmann Tufting AG and Jeremy's little plan with

Philip Ashworth. There were times when Jeremy's capers strained the loyalties, to put it mildly.

But at least life hadn't yet settled to boredom.

Jacques Charville, opposite, was staring at me with his mouth open.

'*Incroyable*,' he moaned. '*Mais vraiment incroyable, Tim.*'

'Nothing personal, you know, Jacques. Just business.'

'But, Tim! The figures. The statistical work. Weeks of work.' He was nearly in tears.

'I know. I really feel for you. Mind you, Janssens isn't far wrong, is he?'

Jacques Charville licked his lips. 'Um, Tim, I don't think I—I mean I work for Eugène—'

'Of course you do. And you've helped prepare his case, eh?'

'Of course.'

'Mmm.' I gave him a meaningful look and he blushed a bit. 'Don't worry, Jacques. Some sort of deal may yet emerge.'

'Oh! I hope so! But not what we had expected. Things look bad, Tim. I mean, we are Malfait's advisers and he was counting on a good deal coming with our help. And our fees; they are linked to the price we can achieve.'

As though I didn't know that! I had no doubt how Eugène Maucourt and Jean Malfait had conducted their strategy. There would, too, be all sorts of backhanders and pay-offs involved, but I didn't want to think about them; they'd only confuse the issue. I'd rather that Eugène Maucourt and Jean Malfait kept their grimy side deals to themselves. My mind needed to be clear of such complications. I stared at Charville for another moment as thoughts flitted about inside my head. Suddenly, even though I didn't know quite what it was for, instinctively I knew what I wanted and I leant across to him.

'Tell me, Jacques; you must have had a lot of access to

Rossignol's private files. Not only facts and figures, but on the experience of the major executives and so on? Personnel files, I mean, Malfait must have them at his central office. A CV for just about all the important people and their personal details?'

A nervous look came back over the table. 'I did. I do have access to all that. In complete confidence, of course.'

'Naturally, Jacques, naturally.' I gave him an encouraging smile. The poor fellow needed a bit of warmth; his side had had rather a dreadful afternoon so far. 'But I wonder —I mean it's no harm now he's dead—could you dig up a bit of information about the late Pierre Martens for me?'

13

Sir Richard was rather miffed when I refused an offer to take his Jaguar after our very hurried post-meeting discussion. I told him that it was far too conspicuous; a rental job was much more my style for these circumstances. At first he was a little bit hurt that I could show that sort of independence towards an offer from someone both senior and close to me and he couldn't quite understand what I meant, but then my methods have always been my own affair and he was still distracted about Janssens and the meeting.

'At least,' he repeated a couple of times, 'Eugène can't accuse *l'Albion perfide* on this occasion. It isn't the Ashworths, and by implication White's, who have sabotaged the deal. This is between Janssens and Malfait. I must say Janssens has behaved very badly. He's strung us all along until the last possible moment and then dropped this little bomb.'

'I take it, from my reading of the various documents, that he hasn't actually committed a penny up to now?'

'Oh no; it's been nothing but declarations of goodwill and cautious statements of intent which are without obligation. The commitment of capital would have followed this.'

'Sounds like the classic ploy of getting to know your competitors' intimate figures by feigning to buy them, to me. One of the oldest tricks in the book. I suppose Malfait and Maucourt's haven't let all the cats out of the bag, have they?'

'Of course not! They're much too canny for that. Janssens has got more than a member of the public, or even a broker's analyst, would get, but he's by no means got the works, I can tell you.'

'And certainly not the Martens material?'

'Indeed not! The general direction and some demonstrations, but not the detail, which is the substance of the investment put in at Wingles and Roubaix. And, come to think of it, Vierzon too.'

'That's interesting. The figure Janssens came up with was about what I'd have said Vierzon was worth on its own.'

Sir Richard gave me a stare. I didn't say anything about the conversation I'd had with François Kolewski in the café. It seemed to me that, like the one with Jeremy in more salubrious and gastronomic circumstances, it was best not thrown in to the line-out just yet. If Janssens wanted to get Vierzon only, or was prepared to pay for that only and scrap the rest, then it confirmed Kolewski's fears about everyone's intentions. He'd asked me to keep a friendly watch on things for Roubaix but I hadn't even opened my mouth, let alone put a word in for him, and I wanted to talk to him, without delay. It looked as though Roubaix was for the chop.

The figure offered made me think that Janssens knew enough about Martens' material to discount it entirely.

On the other hand, Malfait would get his insurance for Wingles and could sell Vierzon, Lens and Roubaix separately if he wanted. He could still do a deal with Janssens on some sort of split-up. There wouldn't be much left in it for Maucourt Frères, though.

'I suppose,' I said carefully to Sir Richard, thinking of Jeremy's providential back-door activities, 'that Ashworths will reconsider the whole Rossignol business if they know that Janssens has come up with this little spanner in the works.'

'Of course. Jack Ashworth'll jump to all sorts of con-

clusions. I want you to get to see him right away, Tim.
Explain to him that the merger is by no means dead. I'll
have to stay here and deal with Eugène and Malfait.'

'OK. I'll go via Lille,' I said.

'What? There's a direct flight to Manchester from Paris.'

'I know. There's one from Lille, too.'

'What on earth d'you want to go via Lille for?'

I grinned at him. 'Trust me. I won't delay long. Just
until tomorrow afternoon.'

'But why? What for?'

I ignored his irritated expression. 'The Duke of Wellington said that time spent on reconnaissance is time well
spent. And his record, in Belgium, is still unbeaten.'

This time I didn't particularly notice the sign for Compiègne or the one for the *Champ de Bataille de la Somme*. I
was driving up the A1 to Lille fast, on my own. I had to
concentrate on other thoughts. It was raw weather, with
sheets of tacky spray coming off the road surface to coat the
windscreen with gunge. I had to keep using the screen
washers. If you're not on the motorways in northern France
you get lumbering farm lorries full of *betteraves*—sugar beet
and mangelwurzels, or root crops like them—spitting mud
at you and blocking the way. On the motorways the heavy
transport includes lots of tankers, the usual Dutch *routiers*
trying to beat it back to Rotterdam in time for a snort of
Oude Genever before supper, but at least you can get past
them, at the expense of another coating of muck. Getting
past them was what I was concentrating on; I wanted to
get to Roubaix before it was too late and I'd left Paris
well after five, cursing at the rush-hour traffic. I'd avoided
phoning Kolewski from Maucourt's and the rental job
didn't have a phone. It would be getting on towards eight
o'clock when I arrived.

In France you get a feeling of distance between towns
that a crowded island like ours doesn't have. The dark

countryside loses all its lights from time to time and you
have a greater sense of being alone. As the evening came
on the traffic thinned and became occasional, although the
route to Lille and Belgium is usually a busy one. I flicked
past the garage-cum-service areas and settled myself to keep
the rental car's speed well up near the ton. Over to my left
was that unhappy stretch of country so fought-over and so
cold; it made me think of Nevinson and then of Sue, at
home in our warm flat in Onslow Gardens, digging up
information for me. So, tomorrow, I hoped Jacques Charville would do the same and relay the result to me via the
Bank. In the gloom of the car's interior I grinned to myself;
here I was, setting people things to find while I hared about
like a blue-arse, buzzing and irritating with noises that,
eventually, someone wouldn't want to hear. Or might swat
at the source of.

It's not a dull life, that's the main thing; dullness kills
quicker than action.

I got to the factory in Roubaix much too late to catch
François Kolewski. Roubaix is impossible to find anything
in if you don't know your way like a local but I was fortunate; a garage man nearby had worked at the carpet mill
and gave me excellent directions. Nevertheless, it was half
past eight by then. I pulled up at the gateman's lodge by
the steel entrance barriers to the Rossignol mill and saw
him look with disdain at my mud-coated car as I clambered
out. Cold damp air hit my unjacketed body and I shivered
as I nipped into his hot little office.

He shook his head emphatically and gestured at the
brightly-lit factory behind us.

'He's gone,' he said. 'Was he expecting you?'

'Unfortunately not. I should have stopped to phone him.
Do you think he went straight home?'

The gatekeeper shrugged. 'Why not? Or he may be out.'

'Where does he live? Near here?'

The gatekeeper looked at me cautiously. 'We're not allowed to give home addresses.'

'I understand that. So let me have your copy of the local telephone directory and I'll look the common French name of Kolewski up in it.'

The gatekeeper grinned and handed it to me. As I took hold of it he said, '19, Rue de la Perche. But you got it from the directory you're holding, not me.'

'Thanks. Can I phone from here? I'll pay, of course.'

'Help yourself.'

There was no answer. Knowing François Kolewski, I guessed he would be downing a beer or two somewhere and my only chance would be to catch him when he finally got home. Or trawl round the local bars.

'Does he live far away?'

'It's on the outskirts. Direction of Wattrelos. Take the next left and go out on the Tourcoing road.'

'Thanks a lot.'

'*Au plaisir.*'

The car looked even filthier in the amber lighting along the pavement. I shivered and put my jacket back on. It took me another ten minutes to sort my way round the edge of Roubaix and I still had to ask again for the Rue de la Perche.

No. 19 was a small terrace house in total darkness. No one answered the bell. With a curse at myself I got back in the car and drove slowly round the block, then diverted towards some lights up the road, where there were shops, life and a bar called guess what, *Le Café des Sports*, how original, but by a miracle Kolewski was coming out of it as I approached. There was no mistaking that huge figure in the shaggy coat, the heavy walk, the battered head.

I couldn't pull up to him because the crossroad lights were at red and I had to sit and fume behind a pick-up truck loaded with broken fridges and ovens while he walked up the road and got into his car, parked near the next junction. Never mind, I thought, all I have to do is follow him home round the next turn and I've got him. He turned to look round as he got in his car and I tried to wave and shout but I was too far back and he didn't give my filthy, muddy car a second glance. He seemed to check round with his gaze and seem satisfied, then he got in his car.

I wondered why he did that; did he think someone might be following him?'

The bloody lights changed at last and the wretched pick-up ground off like a tortoise havering over a lettuce leaf. The only consolation was that I had a view of the next turn, where Kolewski would need to go if he was headed home, so I could follow him quite clearly.

He didn't take it.

Bugger it, I thought, that's typical, he must be going on to eat somewhere if he hasn't already, it's coming up for nine. The pick-up signalled badly, slowed, and turned off the road. Way ahead I saw Kolewski's car and stepped on the gas to get after it.

It is a real jungle of old industrial roads round there. I followed rapidly, realizing that we were working north towards Tourcoing, then started to feel foolish about myself. What would I do when Kolewski stopped? Suppose he was going to meet a girlfriend? I'd look a proper gooseberry, butting in on his evening. I decided to follow more carefully and only approach him, when he stopped, if he obviously stayed alone. That strategy felt more comfortable; I dropped back a bit and let the distance increase between us.

He stopped somewhere in Tourcoing in quite a busy street and parked under some trees where there was a ser-vice road which provided a useful parking area. A smart-looking brasserie, brightly lit, cast coloured light across the cars, so I guessed this was where he'd come to eat and pulled in to the pavement thirty yards short of him.

Kolewski heaved himself out, looked round, took off the huge shaggy coat and threw it into the back of his car. He took out a much smarter camel-hair overcoat, put it on, looked round again, straight past my car, looked the other way, then went to a Peugeot 204, a small black and red GT version, parked four cars along from him, and tapped on the driver's window. In the red and yellow light from the brasserie I saw him smile at the driver.

A blonde head emerged. Thank God, I thought, I didn't muck up his date for the evening. It would have been bloody embarrassing.

The blonde got out and embraced him. In the multi-coloured lights I saw her put her mouth to his and the two of them kissed like people who've been starved of kissing for years, holding each other tight as gorillas.

I sat quite still, frozen white at the wheel of my rental car like a man graven from marble.

François Kolewski put his big flanker's hands under the girl's coat and took hold of parts of her in a way that indicated he was accustomed to taking hold of such parts with joy and a welcome from her. She broke the kiss and put back her head to smile at him as she enjoyed the pre-dinner caresses.

Her face was quite clearly illuminated; I saw it as clear as could be.

She was Elizabeth van Laeten.

14

'Mr Janssens,' his secretary said, with a note of disapproval towards those who, like me, arrived early and unscheduled at his office, 'will not be in until a little later. He did not arrive home from Paris until late last night.'

I nodded sympathetically, wondering what other mischief he'd got up to, which other proposed ventures he might have sabotaged at the last moment.

'I suppose,' she continued dubiously, 'it would be all right if you waited for him. The trouble is we're expecting a group from one of the big German discount chains and Elizabeth van Laeten will be occupied with them in the waiting-rooms downstairs.'

I nodded again sympathetically, thinking that Elizabeth van Laeten might not be quite as bright this morning as on other occasions, not if the nocturnal attentions of a lustful François Kolewski were anything like what they used to be in his rugger-playing days.

'You say you don't want to see any of the managers? Not the computer people or anything?'

'No,' I said, firmly but cheerfully. 'Not the computer people. Just Mr Janssens.'

Especially not the computer people, dear God.

'I see.' She teetered for a moment and then made her decision, smiling at last. 'Well, Mr Janssens did say you and Sir Richard were to be given every facility. Would you like to wait in his office?'

'That's very kind.'

'Would you like some coffee?'

'That would be marvellous.'

It would be marvellous. Anyone who spends most of the

night wide awake appreciates repeated doses of coffee in the morning. Apart from thinking about what I'd seen outside the brasserie in Tourcoing before Kolewski and Elizabeth van Laeten disappeared inside it, I'd tried to read most of Jacques Charville's market research and statistics, without absorbing very much of any of it. My mind was in too much of a turmoil. There was a bit Jacques Charville had dug out from the EIU report—that's the Economist Intelligence Unit's report on household textiles, furnishings and floorcoverings in Europe—that spoke of the increased collaboration between French manufacturers in Lille, Roubaix and Tourcoing with Belgian manufacturers in Kortrijk, or Courtrai if you're French, but I felt somehow that the authors didn't have exchanges of mistresses, or girlfriends, in mind when they wrote it.

Nor, perhaps, the theft of each other's computer development work.

Bob Janssens' office was still very clean and modern, with a desk clear of papers as before, so that his secretary must have been quite happy to leave me in it; no chance of reading any incriminating correspondence here. I wandered over to the big Flemish bureau-bookcase as she brought me in a cup of encouragingly strong coffee.

'A magnificent piece,' I said, sycophantically, looking at its great pot-bellied swell below.'

'Oh yes. It was Monsieur Louis Janssens' own. The father of the current Monsieur Janssens and founder of the firm, before the war.'

'Indeed?'

'Oh yes. He was an exceptional man.'

'I'm sure.'

She indicated the coffee, smiled, and left. I ran my eye along the books behind the glazed doors. There were quite a lot of textile works, technical stuff on wool and fibres and processors, mixed in with business and management theory.

The dyeing of yarns; the spinning of yarns; weaving, tufting and needling. I stifled a yawn and picked up my coffee. There was nothing I wanted to read on these lower shelves; I'd had quite enough facts for the time being.

My eye caught an English Penguin book, higher up, quite an old one: the Penguin Poets; Robert Graves. Aha, I thought, there we are: back to that first morning north of Loos, with Jack Ashworth flapping in the wind and the spire of La Bassée glinting across the fields. Janssens' enthusiasm was carried through to his office, or at least to his father's furniture. Next to it was an older book, thin, a sixpenny job from what looked like the nineteen-twenties: *Robert Graves, a selection of poems*, published by Ernest Benn. Next to that was a very interesting early thing entitled *Fairies and Fusiliers*.

Surely that must be a first edition?

I tested the glazed doors. They were unlocked. With a feeling of clandestine guilt I opened them and took out the slim, stained volume. *Fairies and Fusiliers*, published by Heinemann, 1917. Worth a bob or two, I should think. I opened this, looked inside, flipping through the yellow-brown pages to see two initials—E.A.—inked at the front, put it back, looked similarly inside the Ernest Benn selection and heard the sound of Janssens arriving outside, his voice going hard about something. Quick as I could, I put the whole lot back and closed the bookcase, turning to stand in the middle of the office with my coffee in hand as Janssens came in.

He wasn't pleased to see me. I felt quite sorry for his secretary; she'd obviously done the wrong thing by letting me in. His face didn't brighten as he formally shook hands with me.

'This is a surprise,' he said factually. His tanned skin looked drawn; around the eyes crow's feet etched deep to age his appearance. The friendliness of his first greeting near Loos and the attitude of our last encounter had gone. 'I had not expected you and I'm sorry but we have important visitors here today, from Germany. I have only a few minutes.'

'I must apologize. It wasn't possible to get hold of you after the meeting yesterday. Sir Richard was quite upset. I came in person on his behalf.'

He nodded; for a moment he hesitated, then his manners got the better of him. 'Another coffee?'

'That's kind, but not if you're in a hurry.'

'I need one myself.' A faint smile cracked his stiff expression. 'You may guess that it was not an easy experience for me, either.'

'I'm sure it wasn't.'

He signalled his secretary for coffee, then sat down behind his desk, with a gesture at a spare chair for me. I sat down.

'I have to ask you, as you may expect, how your, er, your re-evaluation of the Rossignol business affects your view of the possible Dillworth Carpet Company participation? Do you still anticipate a joining of interests there?'

He took a sip of coffee, put it down, made sure the secretary had gone and looked at me with hard, bright eyes.

'You smooth bastard,' he said.

'I beg your pardon?'

'I said you smooth bastard. Yes, you. Do you think I don't know the carpet business? Eh? Do you think I'm not dealing, every day, with all the important players in Europe? What do you take us Belgians for? Bloody fools?'

'I'm afraid I'm not with you.'

'You British sit out there on your island and think you can come over here, play on our pitch, and imagine we don't know the game? How do you think Belgium has survived? By being ignorant?'

'This is not informing me of anything.'

'Oh, isn't it? Well, let me inform you, Mr Simpson: my German contacts tell me that the Ashworths are playing games with Hartmann Tufting, and White's are helping them. While their Chairman, that dear ethical gentleman Sir Richard, is dipping into my figures, finding out all about my business by taking advantage of my good faith, all the time you and your London narks are in Frankfurt. You call that good business ethics, do you?'

'I'm afraid I don't know what you're talking about.'

He sneered. 'Oh, don't you? I think you do. I shall be telling Sir Richard, very shortly, precisely what I think of him, you, Maucourt's and the whole slimy gang of you! You're as bad as Malfait, who has tried to pull a fast one, aided and abetted by Eugène Maucourt, who's after a fat fee as usual. I'm not sure that I won't call in the press, not just the press here but your *Financial Times* as well, to tell them just how unethical a game you've been playing. What would you think of that?'

'I wouldn't if I were you.'

'Why the hell not?'

'Because pots look silly calling kettles black.'

His threatening expression flickered. 'What the hell does that mean?'

I ignored the question for the moment. 'Are you telling me you aren't looking at other options while talking to Rossignol and Dillworth's? In quite the normal business manner?'

'No, I'm not!'

I raised my eyebrows. 'You mean you consider Rossignol and Dillworth's to be the only strategic opportunity for Louis Janssens?'

He hesitated slightly. 'Of course not.'

'Then doubtless you too are having exploratory talks with other people while you're manœuvring to get the Vierzon factory you want.'

'Vierzon? Who says I want Vierzon?'

'Now that you've got the guts of Martens' work, what else is there of value in Rossignol?'

His jaw dropped. I knew I'd guessed the situation spot on, just as sure as dropping a chancy goal from way out and surprising yourself as the ball soars between the posts.

'No wonder you avoided my eye yesterday. Martens was going to blow the gaffe, wasn't he? He found out somehow that you'd stolen all his work. Probably copied all the material, the disks and systems files, at Roubaix.' Now it was my turn to stare hard. 'A very convenient fire, that was. And a very convenient death.'

His mouth opened, shut, opened, then clamped tight before he ground out his next words. 'What are you suggesting? Be very careful what you say, *Mister* Simpson!'

'I am being careful. It is a criminal offence to steal industrial secrets. By any method. Martens' were stolen. Or perhaps I should say Rossignol's, because they belong to Malfait, really. I think you've got them. I think Martens was murdered. Strangely convenient, wasn't it, that we were delayed on our way to Wingles? I haven't voiced my suspicions yet but I don't think you're in a position to make accusations about anyone. If you do, I'll come out with it all.'

I stopped there. That would do for the moment. He was going a nasty colour and my own blood pressure wasn't very low.

He stood up, his face working, eyes glittering. 'Get out! Get out of my office! I shall report this to the police! I'm not going to sit here and listen to this!'

I got up, put my cup back on the tray, and walked to the door. The bluebottle had buzzed enough to create anger; now it was time to get ready for the swatting.

Janssens' other connecting door, not to his secretary's

ante-room, swung open and Elizabeth van Laeten burst in, not at first seeing me under the other architrave.

'*Bob, chérie, il faut que tu viens. Les Allemands veulent—*'

She stopped. Her face froze at the sight of me. I wonder, I thought, looking at the slightly puffy swells under her eyes, how many times you've said *chérie* in the last few hours, and how many bosses get called that by their Marketing Directors?

I closed the door carefully behind me.

15

I didn't go straight to the airport at Lille. I drove back along the motorways to Lens. Sir Richard probably wouldn't have been very pleased but I have this thing about sites, about places and their atmospheres, which I have to satisfy. Somehow I feel more confident when I've been there and seen it; this shows a failing in intellectual and imaginative power, perhaps. Or a morbid curiosity.

Lens has a very congested approach as you come close to the town centre, but it's much more open once you're right in. The main street is wide, wide enough for the Town Hall to be set at right angles and for cars to park diagonally all along the pavements. Brick, is the major impression you get, lots of red brick, some of it chequered or diapered and most of it new, in Flemish bond I suppose, even though this is a French city, with modern shops and so on. This had been Martens' home; I wanted a sniff of it because he lived here and went up the road to Wingles from here, every day, day in and day out, for a long time.

He didn't have any family. Did he, then, live like a mouse, stay at home and do his own domestic work, the shy bachelor with an ironing board? Or did he have a married woman somewhere, a girlfriend, a mistress, go to a brothel, was he a regular client, *Bonsoir, Mr Martens, Berthe vous attende comme tous les vendredis?* Or did he pick up tarts near the railway station and have them service him in his car for a cheap thrill? Did he have any desires at all? Was he a poof?

He must have had some sort of life apart from data processing and systems design, damn it.

I telephoned Jacques Charville at Maucourt's in Paris and got Martens' address from him.

'Tim.' Charville was apologetic. 'I haven't had time to get the other information you asked for. I'll fax it to London for you tomorrow. It's been bedlam here, as you can imagine. Eugène's in a hell of a mood. He and Malfait have been discussing other approaches, other amalgamations. I've been running like a hare. Digging up facts on just about every carpet firm in Belgium and France.'

'I understand, Jacques. Thanks a lot.'

I didn't ask why he wasn't digging up facts on German carpet companies, or Italian ones or, come to that, the British. We all have our own versions of insularity and language dictates one of them.

Martens lived in a flat not far from the town centre. There was just a door, varnished and locked, with a bell beside it. I rang the bell but no one came, no tearful woman or defensive male friend. No one. The door was unresponsive. From here he must have walked out to do his shopping or gone to cafés and restaurants to eat *frites* and drink beer. Now he was dead. There wasn't a bit of him left. Just some traces in French police laboratories, enough to satisfy a coroner; that had been established. He was dead all right; this wasn't a disappearing act, a John Stonehouse job, Martens had been fried to less than Jeremy's crisp. Eradicated. Not even a skeleton to tell if he'd been hit over the head or tied up before the factory went up in smoke. Just traces.

Traces, I supposed, were more than was left of a lot of the soldiery who visited this region. Along with quite a few civilians, too.

I went to the local newspaper office and asked to talk to someone about the fire, anyone who'd covered it. The journalist who'd been involved was out but there was a girl-editor, pleasant and friendly, who chatted to me. No, they hadn't got a photograph of Martens. No, they hadn't found a girlfriend or an ex-wife or anything like that. The

fire was quite big news locally because of employment but
the girl was a bit cynical, like Kolewski. There'd been more
than one factory fire in the last year or two. Times were
hard. The girl sub-editor cocked a significant eyebrow. But
Martens: no, there was nothing much about him. Lived
quietly, worked hard, tended to go regularly to a particular
brasserie, where he'd read the newspaper with his evening
meal. Liked a beer. When it came to football he supported
Ghent. A bit reclusive.

What did I expect? A scoop?

He was late for work on the morning of the fire, I said
to the girl, I just wondered why. He was normally there
promptly at eight but that morning he didn't get in until
well after nine, maybe nine-thirty. Anyone know anything
about that?

Not much, the girl said, but they did more or less agree
that he was at the main post office about eight-thirty to
nine that day, buying some stamps and posting a letter or
letters. The postman who delivers to his street was there
and saw him, waved him good-morning. Everyone said how
awful, see, regardless of his fate the local victim posts, or
posted.

Letters? Any idea where to?

None, the girl said, no, postage for the Common Market
is the same uniform rate all over so you couldn't tell from
the stamps. He'd have to have shown the letter to someone.
Why, what is all this about, something we should know?
Something sinister?

Oh no, I said, just filling in a few gaps for the insurance
and company pension fund, all that sort of thing, thanks
very much. I grinned at her and left.

A man, a manager with a perfectly good office postal
department at work, a man who could conveniently pop
anything in with the company post there and then, makes
himself late by waiting for the main post office to open

and sending off something that wasn't local. Something he obviously didn't want anyone at the office to see.

Nothing sinister in that?

I'd hate to be a policeman.

I drove back to Lille and waited irritably for a plane to Manchester. The trouble with real life is that events and information never coincide nice and cleanly. We can all of us win the great battles of history with hindsight fed by knowing the sequence of events and the strength of the opposing forces, but the difficulty at the time was that you didn't know the half of it and the events often didn't oblige by happening the way you might expect. Wellington, from reconnaissance, was a dab hand at guessing what was over the hill and even he wasn't on his best form at Waterloo. As for me and over the hill, or the moors, I wasn't doing too much guessing because I felt I didn't have enough information, even though what I'd got looked pretty obvious.

I was too late into Manchester Airport to catch Jack Ashworth at his Darwen mill so I stayed the night at the Last Drop motel village on the withering slope above Bolton. The wind took the central fountain by the throat and shot it horizontally across the lawn until someone had the wit to turn it off, but the dinner was excellent and I could amuse myself watching some locals, dressed to the nines, observing the conventions by ordering Sauternes with their steak while downing frequent pints of bitter, which was what they really wanted. It reminded me of Nevinson's regrets about the healthy philistinism of the British being adulterated by Nanny BBC; it cheered me up to think that all those decades of prim BBC intonations have had such little effect on honest, full-blooded vulgarity.

I called Sue and had a long, rather emotional conversation to assure her with some amusement that I was safely stuck out on a Lancashire hillside, not skulking around the

dark Satanic mills of northern France, pursued by arsonists.
She mentioned that she'd talked to an R.A. friend who
recalled a Nevinson of a French scene from a window going
for £36,000 somewhere, but it was still hardly in the Impres-
sionist class. The R.A. friend said he thought that it was
awfully cheap. Sue said she thought the same. Could the
one that Jack Ashworth had be a fake? It could, I said, but
I'd hardly buy it without having it checked and since he
claimed to have the original invoice from the Leicester Galleries its provenance seemed flawless. I've never heard of
anyone faking a Nevinson but who knows, it could happen.
My gut feeling was that Ashworth's painting was genuine.

She then issued an ultimatum to meet her next day and
stuck to it despite my protests of being extremely busy.
There are times when Sue is adamant, regardless of Belgians, Frenchmen or imperious Whites and this, evidently,
was one of them. We then exchanged loving and entirely
private messages, one of which would, I hoped, make her
blush, and I put the phone down.

The painting was still on view in Jack Ashworth's office
when I breezed in first thing the next morning. The soldiers
were marching on towards their next lethal engagement but
he was massed behind his great mahogany desk, with
papers and bits of carpet piled high in front of him.

'I've been expecting you,' he rumbled, almost accusingly.
'A bit before, like. Even yesterday.'

'Really? What made you expect me then?'

'A little bird. A little bird with a knighthood. Rang me
up to ask were you here.'

'Did he now? Didn't say why, did he?'

'No, he didn't. Seemed a bit put out, I'd say, that you
weren't. Said you should have been, yesterday after.'

'Oh? Did he say what for? I mean what I'd he here for?'

'Oh, aye, he told me a bit about it. Seems that that
Janssens has put spanner in t'works, has he?'

'Something like that.'

Ashworth grinned. 'Doesn't surprise me,' he growled. 'Our Philip said as how he reckoned Janssens were a fast bugger. Smooth, ain't he? Going on about poets and that. Still, you can't blame him for trying. Trade's trade, after all. No one gets owt for nowt.'

'I thought you were quite keen on his outfit.'

'I am. I am that. But not at any price. Not likely. He's trying to get Rossignol cut-price but he'll get short answer from me if he tries that on here.'

'I don't think he'd do that.'

'No? Why not? What a man does in one place he'll do in another. Always remember that.'

'Question of circumstances,' I murmured. And reaction, I thought to myself. Janssens might rely on a cool French treatment of his offer, even a pretty mixed one from Malfait, but from Ashworth he'd be damn certain what retort he'd get, let alone the chance of a thick ear.

'So what did he say?' Ashworth's voice cut through my thoughts.

'Who? Oh, Janssens. You mean when I saw him?'

'Aye.'

'How do you know I saw him?'

'For God's sake. You went up to that area, didn't you? That's what Sir Richard said, any road. What else would you be doing? I got the impression that Janssens had been bending his ear. Your trip seems to have taken you a bit longer than he thought it would. And not been quite what he'd expected.'

'Ah. Wasn't it? Sorry. Er, well, Janssens said that was his offer and he didn't care to make any other.'

'Oh aye?'

'Yes.' I decided that with Ashworth bulls were best taken by the horns and nettles firmly grasped. 'He wasn't too pleased about your conversations with Hartmann Tufting, either.'

Ashworth's expression changed. A twinkle came into his eye. 'Oh? How did he know about that?'

'Trade contacts. He does a lot of business in Germany.'

'I bet he does. No, I don't suppose he was too chuffed. Nor was your Sir Richard.'

'Oh Lord. You've told him?'

'I have that. After Janssens had, it looks like. It seemed to me it was better to be all above board with our own bankers. I didn't realize that you and Jeremy White were —what? keeping him in the dark, like?'

'Didn't you? I wonder if Philip hadn't told you anything about that?'

Ashworth's twinkle spread from his eyes to draw his face into a broad smile. 'Maybe,' he said. 'I must say it's nice to know that other firms have their internal dissensions. Even merchant bankers. Our lot have always been an argumentative family. Lots of disagreement, there is.'

'It's bit unfortunate as far as the Bank goes. I mean, what you must think of the way we work. And Janssens is threatening to tell the world about bad faith and so on.'

Ashworth kept his smile. 'Nay, lad, never mind what folks think. A bit of argufying is good for a firm. Keeps folks on their mettle. Your Sir Richard and Jeremy'll be better for a bit of friction. As for Janssens, he won't shout too loud. Never does any good to wash dirty linen in public.'

'So are you serious about Hartmann Tufting?'

'They're not bad for a bunch of Huns. Philip's quite impressed. Once he's done his estimate of what it'll cost to complete that Martens' work he'll call a meeting and we'll make a decision, never fear. He's got one more visit to Germany—it's to a mill of theirs near Aachen somewhere —then he'll have everything he needs.'

'So it will be either Janssens, or Rossignol, or Hartmann,

or some sort of combination depending on Philip's work and the normal commercial factors we'll help you with?'

'That's it.'

'Quite an important role he's playing.'

'He is that. Quite right, too.'

My eye strayed to the Nevinson. 'Tell me, who brought Philip up? After his father's death, I mean.'

Jack Ashworth looked surprised. 'His mother, of course. Who else?'

'His mother?'

'Aye. Our Betty. Grand girl, she is. She were one of the Dillworth family actually. The original owners we married into and bought out. Distantly, of course; she were a very distant cousin. Retired long since; in her seventies now. Bought her a nice place at Southport. Our family look after their own, you know.'

'Did she ever marry again?'

He shook his head. 'Never. It were a terrible thing, losing Ted like that. He used to be at Squire's Gate—Blackpool —before he got promoted and they moved him to Norfolk. He were posted missing at first. His plane came down on the way back from a raid on Hamburg. Lancaster, as I've told you. They survived, the crew. We had a note smuggled across to say they were in the hands of the Resistance. In Belgium. They were way off course because of damage but they all got out. It were 1944 and the Hun was on the run. Betty was beside herself. Philip was only one year old. If they could hide long enough everything would be all right.' He shook his head. 'The Huns got them somehow. Betrayed, they were. Shot while trying to escape was the excuse.' His battered face darkened. 'Murdered, of course. They say all's fair in love and war but I don't think so. Bitter, it was. We got the news at the end of 1944. I was only eleven then and he would have been twenty-one. Anyway, Betty devoted herself to Philip. Never married again.

And he's a bright lad. She's always been proud of him. Rightly so; he's a credit to her. Got his own family and she's got grandchildren, so all's well really.' He frowned at me. 'I'm not sure what all this has to do with anything.'

'Sorry, I just wondered how the family structure went.' I stared across at the Nevinson. 'It was you talking about your grandfather originally that got my interest. The one who bought that painting.'

'Aye?'

'Yes. You see, I got confused. You said he bought that from the Leicester Galleries at an exhibition which must have been in September or October 1916.'

'He did. We've got invoice to prove it.'

'But the Accrington Pals were decimated on the Somme in July of that year.'

'Of course they were. And my grandfather was with them. That was the whole point. He survived the first week of the Somme—the most dangerous thing you think of— only to be killed later. That's why they think that painting's bad luck.'

I swallowed. 'I see. When did your grandfather get killed, then?'

'In 1917. Late 1917. That's why I don't hold with the family's bad luck story. My grandfather was killed on the Somme in 1917. After all, fighting went on there right to the end of the war.'

'Oh.'

A look of incomprehension came into his face. 'What did you think? That I was having you on?'

'No, no, of course not. I just got confused on my dates, that's all. Of course the fighting went on.' A sudden thought struck home: 1917. 'Tell me: what was your grandfather's Christian name?'

Jack Ashworth stared at me strangely. 'Edwin,' he said. 'Why?'

'So his initials—'

The telephone in front of him rang. Ashworth lifted it irritably, then his expression softened. He passed the receiver across. 'It's for you,' he said. 'Your London office. After the naughty truant, they are.'

I took the phone. It was Jeremy's secretary, Laura. 'Tim? Found you at last. Can you come to a meeting at the Bank this afternoon? Jeremy and Sir Richard want to see you.' Her voice wavered into a suppressed giggle. 'I think they have a lot to say to you. Both of them. Jeremy actually asked me to tell you that something solid has hit the rotary device. Those were his words. Oh, and there's a fax for you from Jacques Charville.'

'Read it out.'

She read it out: Pierre Martens was brought up by foster parents in Ghent. Both now dead. But his birth was registered in Roeselare in 1944.

'Roeselare?'

'That's what it says, Tim.'

Roeselare; a small town north-west of Courtrai.

'Tim?'

'Yes?'

'What time shall I say you'll meet Sir Richard and Jeremy this afternoon?'

I looked across at Jack Ashworth, who was grinning at me faintly. Lancastrians do enjoy a bit of the dramatic aggro.

'Tell them,' I said wearily, 'that I'll be there by three. I have to get to a much more important engagement before then.'

16

'I do not want to hear,' Sue said, as she handbagged the change for the tickets from the office under the portico at the Imperial War Museum, 'that you ought, really, to be at the Bank, or in France, or Belgium or somewhere. Or, indeed, in Sidi Barrani. Or anywhere like it. Not even Lancashire. I ought, come to that, to be at work in my office, too. There are some important matters I have to deal with today. You may not think so, but there are.'

'I'm sure there are, Sue.'

'I don't know why it is that you convey the impression that what you do is somehow more important than what I do.'

'I'm sorry, Sue. I really cannot imagine how that should come about.'

She smiled and put her tongue out at me. In front of the museum, along the Lambeth Road, traffic whisked by oblivious of the two huge naval guns trained to fire nonchalantly over vehicle roofs and into the centre of London. A graffitied section of the Berlin Wall stood silent behind its explanatory plaque, an example to the hordes of potentially aerosol-armed schoolchildren who flood the museum at regular intervals. The weather was cold and grey. It was a weekday morning at its twelve o'clock incoherence; not a very busy time for the Imperial War Museum. The visit had been sprung on me quite suddenly by Sue during our telephone conversation and she was in a determined mood. Protests that it might be better to wait until the weekend had been dismissed intransigently. Sue was clearly anxious to resolve some aspect or another that she felt it necessary to resolve here and now, probably for my protection. For this reason I refrained from pointing out that a curator from the Tate Gallery might quite validly visit the modern British art in the galleries at the Imperial War Museum as part of her work whereas a banker, even a banker who equally administered an art fund but who was supposed to be dealing with the difficulties of carpet company mergers and their attendant incendiaries in Europe, quite apart from running between Manchester and a potentially unpleasant meeting, might find such truancy harder to justify. Rational arguments of that sort would simply cause trouble.

In any case, I was curious.

We entered the large glass doors and went into the main hall, to be confronted by a variety of lethal vehicles, guns, rockets and fighter aeroplanes slung at angles overhead. A very large, charming double-decker bus of pre-1914 vintage, with an outside staircase and dated advertisements stuck on its crimson livery, stood solemnly in the centre. Old Whatsitsname, which was used in 1914 or 1915 to carry troops to the front, had come to rest in a place of honour. We passed this and headed for the staircase at the back, where the enormous nose and cockpit of a Lancaster bomber, cut through the section and staircased so that you could mount and inspect the interior with its offset pilot's seat in every detail.

'The First World War gallery is up the left,' Sue said firmly, seeing me look wistfully at the Lancaster. 'The Second World War is to the right, but we won't be going into that. Follow me.'

We mounted the stairs and, at the top, turned resolutely left. There was another pair of glass doors, lighter this time, to go through and there we were, into the First World War gallery.

They were all on parade: the Nashes, Augustus John, Wadsworth, Orpen, Eric Kennington's *The Kensingtons at*

Laventie, Sargent, Stanley Spencer, the whole lot. There were long days of viewing here if you felt inclined to do it properly. In a sense I was sad to see them all tucked away like this, comfortably and competently pensioned-off into a specialist gallery of war paintings rather than mixed-in with the rest of life's experiences in a general exhibition. But it was understandable, even correct. Specializations are specializations in everything: this was what the museum was for.

'First,' Sue said briskly, 'we'll look at those which are out now. Then we'll go through the video display. Come on, through here.'

We passed through the first area of gallery—past Paul Nash's *The Menin Road*, tree-stumped and puddled, then John Nash's *Over the Top*, all puttees and bodies in white snow above the brown-red gash of trench—to reach a large square painting of spiky soldiers clumped in a mob, sitting or standing in attitudes of disorientation and blank fatigue.

'Nevinson,' I said.

'Well done. It's called *After a Push*.'

'It's excellent.'

'It's not just excellent, it's brilliant. Look at the composition, the grouping of those soldiers on the left, and the spacing. Now come and look at the other one they have on display.'

We moved across the gallery to a smaller painting, a Cubist gouache of marching French soldiers in blue coats and red trousers, their uniforms and heads mottled with képis, frying pans and packs. Their guns were long black spikes slanting up leftwards to counterbalance their black boot-legs, curving and slanting down rightwards to give an impression of powerful movement, almost stroboscopic blurring, a rapid tramp of heavy feet on the march.

'That,' I said, 'is very similar to the one in Jack Ashworth's office at Darwen. Very similar indeed.'

'Probably a study for *Column on the March*.' Sue nodded, with satisfaction. 'I thought you might be pleased to see it. It's almost a sketch, but what movement he's got!'

I raised my eyebrows. Sue is not often enthusiastic about the paintings I get involved with. Her remarks about the machine-gunner at the Hayward, not so far away, hadn't been very complimentary. Now she seemed more than a little bit keen.

'It's not fair,' she said.

'What's not fair?'

'Nevinson. Did you know that he shared a studio with Modigliani?'

'I had heard,' I said carefully, 'something to that effect.'

'Come and look at the videos.'

The Imperial War Museum has installed a splendid video disc system which is absolutely free of charge and saves you hours of search. There in the upper foyer you stand in front of a telly screen and scan a pictorial set of filing cabinets. When the first letter of the surname of the artist you want comes up you press the button and, on the screen, the filing cabinet drawer opens. Paintings which aren't out on display in the galleries can be looked at easily like this.

We scrolled our way along to Nevinson and in no time I was looking at *The Road from Arras to Bapaume*.

Sue shivered. 'Isn't it awful? Desolate, a wasteland. And the road, going on and on to nowhere like that. He certainly could convey the results of war. But this isn't one of the 1915–16 ones which Rothenstein raves about. They were all taken from his experiences in Belgium. This must have been done after his second visit, when he was in France as well. It's not Cubist either; it's primitive, almost naïve. Tiny dark figures, almost like L. S. Lowry ones much later. Empty, destroyed.' She shivered again. 'I'm not sure I

agree with Rothenstein. This may not be like his first exhibition but it's still very dramatic.'

I put my hands in my pockets. Like Sue, I'd read Sir
John Rothenstein's essay on Nevinson in his *Modern English
Painters*. In fact, I'd re-read it before going to look at *La
Mitrailleuse*, which Nevinson actually painted during his
two-day honeymoon in 1915. I remembered the remarks
about his sense of the hostility of the art establishment, his
persecution by Tonks, the great teacher at the Slade, who
behaved abominably. But most of all I remembered
Rothenstein's awful judgement: the 1915 paintings were
great, to be classified among the very best of anyone's, but,
with a few exceptions, for another thirty years of painting
it was downhill all the way. At twenty-seven he had done
his best; that made me shiver, more than the images of war.

'You've been doing your homework,' I said to Sue.

'Yes, I have.' Under her wavy brown hair her face had
gone serious. Her large blue eyes looked up from the screen
to mine with troubled uncertainty in them. 'I've done a lot,
Tim. I even bought a copy of Nevinson's autobiography,
Paint and Prejudice, from your old bookseller friend, Mr
Goodston of Praed Street.'

'Really? How is dear Mr Goodston?'

'Betting as badly as ever. On the slowest horses in England, he says. But he sent you his very best wishes and
wanted to know when you'd next be in to snap up his stock.'

'Good old Mr Goodston.'

'When I asked for the Nevinson he pulled a face. He got
it out, said that it's a steady seller, charged me thirty
pounds and tendered a little nugget of advice.'

'What was that?'

'Nevinson, he said, in that funny ruminative way of his,
Nevinson: your husband is as contrary to current vogue as
ever. That is to the good. I hope, he said, I hope, however,
that young Mr Simpson will not find, as Nevinson did, that

his finest hour was in warfare and that peace brings nothing but neglect.'

'Wise old Mr Goodston. I think he's got it wrong, though, like Rothenstein. Nevinson did rather well during the peace. Hindsight may say he didn't paint masterpieces, but he led a pretty hectic and enjoyable life. Lots of bohemian parties.'

'I have also been to beard Charles. In his Bond Street lair.'

'Good heavens, Sue, you're doing all the things I normally reserve for myself. What's caused all this?'

'I asked you if you wanted me to help and you said yes. So, since you've been away a lot, I've done it.'

'Well, I'm grateful.'

She crooked a smile. 'I was curious.'

Her face was still troubled and uncertain. Sue takes artists seriously, and I knew what she was feeling, but Nevinson is long dead and it's idle to repine. I put my arm around her and said, 'Come on, the coffee shop will be open. Let's go down there and you can tell me all about it over a cuppa and a cream bun.'

She grimaced. Sue, like all women these days, is on a diet. Cream buns are not on the Approved List.

Back down the stairs we went and I couldn't help it; on the way past the Lancaster I nipped across to look in. When I was at school we had an inspired English master called Dan Dickey who'd been a Lancaster pilot, trained in Texas, got shot down over Germany, had wonderful stories to tell. I've always had a thing about Lancasters. Like nearly everyone else I know.

Sue pulled another face. 'Tim! We're not here to play bomber pilots.'

Contritely I got the coffee and sat across the table from her in the empty café. She put sweetener in hers and sipped ruminatively before she began. I looked at her sympathetically.

'He was an awkward squad, wasn't he?' I spoke gently. 'Nevinson, I mean. Embarassing, too. Those later paintings called *Pan Triumphant* or *The Twentieth Century*—embarassing fantasies that confirmed his critics' suspicions. He was difficult to slot. Didn't fit. Son of a real Hampstead pair: a jingoistic journalist war correspondent father who was a fervent Socialist, and a bluestocking suffragette mother who ran round London with young lad Nevinson on Mafeking Night, ringing a handbell. Like a caricature from Peter Simple. They were artistic with a capital A. His schooldays were terrible. Bullying and sleaze. He had a persecution complex. But he was the classic art student: the Slade, Paris pre-1914, he knew all the great Continental artists. Ground that into the British artists' faces a bit, I imagine.'

'Tonks,' Sue said, drawing her mouth into a line, 'told him he was unsuited to be an artist while he was at the Slade and advised him to quit. A young insecure student like that, who was clearly very talented, being told that, by so powerful a figure? Nevinson dropped out in despair for a while and went into journalism. Until now I've admired Tonks, the great Slade teacher. Now I detest the name.' Her eyes flashed. 'Do you know that for years after the Tate had acquired *La Mitrailleuse*, Tonks campaigned to get them to throw it out? I mean, not content with nearly destroying Nevinson psychologically, he then hounded him throughout his career? How could he do that?'

'Tonks had his pet hates. The art establishment has a nasty history for some painters.'

'You haven't read Nevinson's book. Tim, he was in on some of the great movements in art. And the rest. Damn it, he even met Lenin in Paris before Lenin was called Lenin. He knew everyone from Severini and Marinetti to Wyndham Lewis.'

'Fell out with them all.'

'That's not true! Modigliani was a friend until he died.

And Orpen. And many others. He gave famous parties. He was the old outgoing type who loved society and music halls and outside life. He couldn't believe how BBC radio was turning a robust brawling nation into a bunch of prim stay-at-homes. You can't help liking him from his book, even though it's full of hobby-horses.'

'Nevinson's experience in journalism taught him how to play the media. He got a lot of publicity. People hated that. Ironically, if it hadn't been for Tonks he might not have got the experience. He was always getting coverage. It got up other artists' noses.'

'Well, they've got their revenge.'

I put my head to one side. 'Revenge? What do you mean?'

She opened her handbag and got out a sheet of paper. 'I went to see Charles for you.'

She was referring to Charles Massenaux, a director of Christerby's specializing in modern painting, an old chum of both mine and hers.

'So you said. And how was Charles?'

'Never mind how Charles was. Charles never changes, you know that. I made him go through his records.'

'His auction records? But I could have done that, Sue.'

'I know you could! But you're not here at present, are you? You're always somewhere else. And I'm saving you time.'

'Sorry. Sorry. Won't interrupt again.'

She smiled. 'Don't. I'm trying to concentrate for you. The fact is, Tim, I can't see why anyone would bother to get criminal in a big way over a Nevinson.'

'Eh?'

'I mean, I just don't see why they should.'

'But I've never suggested they are.'

She waved that aside. 'You know very well how you've got into hot water over things like this in the past. Well,

Charles gave me a list of the Nevinsons sold at auction over
the last year or five. And none of them went over £20,000,
not even a rather good war one of 1916 called *Motor Transport*, although that's from his second show, not the first
famous one.'

'Maybe he's due for a revival. You did say that one had
gone for £36,000 sometime.'

She shook her head vigorously. 'One of the paintings
Rothenstein says he most admires, apart from the war
paintings, is *Henley Regatta*, with its night-time colour
effects. Well *Henley Regatta* came up at Sotheby's last Nov-
ember and the estimate was £12,000 to £15,000. Even at
that price it didn't sell. It was brought in at £9,000.' She
stared at me mournfully across the café table. 'No one
would bid any higher. If a Nevinson was worth a fortune I
could understand this whole affair turning into one of your
dreadfully murderous capers, but it isn't. Worth a fortune,
I mean.'

I stared out through the long window-paned doors of the
café to the cluster of lethal machinery outside. From where
I was sitting I could just see the bulbous crystal nose of the
Lancaster and above it a First World War biplane, forever
suspended in pristine, cleanly safety.

'So you've eliminated the idea of a Nevinson being some
sort of bait.'

'Yes.' Her voice was firm. 'People might just murder for
a painting worth up to £10,000 or so, but they're not the
high-finance types you've talked of on this jaunt.'

'That lets out the Ashworths, you think?'

'Yes.'

'Even though Jack Ashworth admits he put that Nevinson up only a few days before I appeared on the scene?'

'Yes.'

I sighed. 'To be fair, he has explained that his grandfather wasn't killed with the Accrington Pals on the Somme

in July 1916. So he could have attended Nevinson's exhibition at the Leicester Galleries the following September-October, when he is said to have bought the painting. He wasn't killed until 1917.'

'Yes.'

'But Philip Ashworth has openly urged me to take the painting off the family's hands.'

Sue hesitated, then shook her head. 'There must be another explanation.'

'Right.'

'I'm sorry, but I can't think of it. I've done as much as I can.'

'Sue, you have saved me a great deal of work.' I stood up. 'I am very grateful. I will have to think about all this very carefully.'

I didn't want to remind her that murder is more often committed for emotional reasons than for monetary gain.

She watched me; she was still sitting down. 'What are you going to do now?'

'I was wondering,' I said, 'whether, as a measure of gratitude, I could buy you lunch?'

She smiled sweetly.

'I,' she said, 'am dieting.'

I smiled back down at her.

'Moules marinières and white wine counts as dieting.'

Her smile broadened. 'Do you know,' she said, 'I do believe that those are on my Approved List.'

17

I arrived at the Bank in a splendid mood. Despite the threat of an unpleasant and acrimonious meeting, with myself the football between the opposed forces of Jeremy and Sir Richard, mussels and white wine with Sue had given me a lift, a sort of boost into surreality. Visions of lowering skies over old battlefields, ugly expressions of anger and the grey ashes of murderous fires had somehow blended into a rosy haze, a tolerantly objective regard for the machinations of Frenchmen, Belgians and Lancastrians locked into the warp and woof of cut-throat carpet competition, as might a deity quaffing champagne from a horned vessel look down upon the scurryings of mere mortals. It was partly wine-induced, in any case, and partly Sue-induced, since, once rid of the research into Nevinson which had been occupying her mind, she was in relaxed and sparkling form. The danger, she obviously concluded, did not come from some-one attempting skulduggery with a painting destined for the Art Fund. This put matters out of her hands. In the past Sue has been more than casually involved in such dangers; business, however, she sees as something way beyond her influence, something simply to be fatalistic about. The load had been taken from her.

She had me in stitches over the arrangements for an exhibition at a provincial gallery which had gone horribly wrong and in which a scarlet nude by Matthew Smith had been hung upside down on opening day. The sudden swap from the tension of Paris, Lille and Courtrai to Sue's gig-gling infection was highly contagious; I forgot all my worries for a glorious hour in her company and sailed into the offices on a high tide of humour.

To my surprise, I found Jeremy, initially, in an equally post-lunch euphoria.

'Everyone,' he said, leaning nonchalantly against the mantelpiece over his office fireplace, 'appears to be getting into a filthy temper about everything. I really do deplore that sort of thing. Really I do.'

'I know, Jeremy.' I made an expansive gesture.' As a man of equable temperament, I am with you in this.'

'You can talk! My goodness! You! You've got a filthy temper. Absolutely manic. I must say that it makes a change, just for once, not to be dealing with one of the results of your violent disposition. Not that this new complaint about you isn't severe. Very severe. Janssens expressed himself most forcefully, as I understand it. Threatened to sue. To plaster our name with scandal. Said you were not only rude but slanderous. Or was it libellous?'

'Libel is to do with the written word, Jeremy. Slander is verbal.'

'Thank God for that. Anyway, Uncle Richard is on his way here post haste. He's taken it all very badly. Especially not being able to contact you.' He frowned at me from below the marine painting over the fireplace. 'It's a pity I had to confirm over the telephone that Janssens' accusations about the Germans were correct. He'd had the news from Jack Ashworth, too. A bit awkward, that. Would have preferred to tell him myself. All in due time, of course. When the moment was ripe.'

'Naturally.'

'Don't smirk!'

'I am not smirking.'

'Smirking is precisely what you are doing, Tim. You accuse Janssens of murder in the pursuit of industrial espionage, you swan about all over Belgium spending money on chips and beer, you act utterly irresponsibly, you arrive up at Darwen a day late, and then you come in here and smirk. Simply because you managed to keep the Hartmann approach secret at the Paris meeting, didn't go bursting out with it to all and sundry, you think you're entitled to smirk. You've got a lot to explain. Let me tell you—' he held up a long forefinger and pointed it at me— 'if you hadn't gone upsetting Janssens like that, he'd never have phoned Uncle Richard and the cat would still be in the bag. Think of that. Utterly thoughtless, that.'

I gritted my teeth. 'Jeremy, quite apart from the Ashworths telling Richard independently of me, your behaviour in all this has been abominable. I am warning you that there is a limit to what I can—'

'There you are! Look at you! Going red! You've got a bad temper, Tim. I've always said—'

'Jeremy! You are a duplicitous swine!'

'And you ruined a perfect lunch! There are not enough lunches left, Tim, in this life, to ruin one like that. It was on its way to immortality and you spoilt it.'

He paused to get his breath back, then he couldn't help it: he grinned at me broadly. I couldn't resist grinning back. Then we both burst out laughing. I suppose that due to past history Jeremy and I can never really fall out too seriously. He's impossible, of course, and has an infuriating habit of doing precisely the reverse of what he has previously been advocating, but I've learnt to cope with that. A man who gives me the scope Jeremy allows deserves tolerance, especially when the scope leads, as it has in the past, to situations needing courage for him to face.

Fortunately we had both composed ourselves by the time Sir Richard White arrived. I wasn't looking forward to the initial part of the encounter, guilt being my prevalent feeling. Sir Richard has been very kind to me, even though he's quite ruthless about using my services in tricky places and we have started a close relationship which he deliberately fosters. In many ways he represents better opportunities and much more mature developments than Jeremy is likely to offer, but old habits die hard; Jeremy and I both have atavistic tendencies.

Sir Richard came in quietly enough, shook both our hands soberly and accepted an offer of coffee, but his manner was tense. When the coffee had been served he went straight to the point, directing his first remarks to me.

'Where the blazes have you been?'

'In Belgium, Richard. As I told you, doing reconnaissance.'

'How much have you known of this German business? Did you know at the time of our last meeting, in Paris?'

'Yes, I did.'

His mouth opened. I felt bloody. The look he gave me had pain as much as anger mixed in it.

'Richard, I guessed the day before our meeting. I wasn't in a position to tell you.'

'Tim's right,' Jeremy intervened quickly. 'I swore him to silence. It was fortunate that Philip Ashworth insisted that his separate approach be kept from the Janssens–Rossignol negotiations and that I assist him independently. I was put into a difficult position. I must apologize to you, Richard, for the difficulty it has caused. I should, perhaps, have refused.'

Sir Richard turned to focus on his nephew. 'Of course you should! How could you have agreed to such a thing?'

Jeremy raised his eyebrows. 'A client is a client. If separate approaches were to be made, it was essential we were involved in the picture. Otherwise we wouldn't justify our fees.'

His uncle bridled. 'You know very well that negotiations were in the final stages in Belgium. No matter what Malfait might do, we had had positive discussions with Janssens. Up to that point, anyway. Now the whole thing is prejudiced. A splendid opportunity has almost certainly been lost, irrevocably.'

Jeremy gaped at him in what seemed like genuine astonishment. 'Oh, come on, Richard, the Ashworths have never been serious about the Janssens connection. They don't trust Belgians as far as they can throw them. Surely you knew that?'

He threw this staggering remark out without the slightest hesitation, as he might a matter of public knowledge, so that the expressions of shock that Sir Richard and I emitted took him quite aback. He hastened to confirm his off-the-cuff assessment.

'Because of the war.' Jeremy was emphatic. 'Philip's father was betrayed by one of them. They've never forgotten it. Philip turned down an invitation to sail there when we were at college. I remember that particularly.'

Jack Ashworth's remarks of the previous day started to sink in. A fast bugger, he'd called Janssens; Ashworth wasn't surprised by his tactics at all.

'But surely they realize that he must have been helped by Belgians as much as the opposite? Belgian Resistance must have been responsible for hiding him? It was the Germans who killed him, damn it, not the Belgians.'

'Of course. But that's the whole point, Tim. If you've been betrayed, whom do you trust and who not? An island foreigner can't tell. So in the Ashworths' minds you don't trust any of them.'

'Great Scott.' Sir Richard's voice had gone almost shrill. 'Do you mean to tell me that I've been working like mad at this affair while the whole time the Ashworths never had the slightest intention of participating in a Belgian joint venture? They're just playing along to find out what information they can?'

'I'm afraid so, Richard. Business is business to the Ashworths.'

'But the Germans? They don't trust old allies like the Belgians but they do trust the Germans? I mean, this is incredible. Fifty years on and we're still like this?'

'Oh, they think they know where they are with the Germans. They can deal with them, given adequate armament and a squadron of dragoons. But not the Belgians. Can't separate the sheep from the goats, you see. And I mean Brussels is synonymous with everything unpleasant nowadays, isn't it?'

'My God.'

There was a silence. The tolerant modern-Continental approach of Sir Richard White, a man who had been more involved in war than any of us but was now almost completely assimilated by the current conception of the Community, was shaken to the core. His eyes met mine in shock as well as speculation. I managed to meet his gaze without blinking and was about to speak, but Jeremy intervened.

'I have to tell you, Richard, that Tim has behaved impeccably as far as our internal affairs are concerned. I thought I had kept the German approach from him completely, but alas, his usual detection did not fail him. He found out the day before yesterday. Despite my concealment.'

'But didn't tell me.' Sir Richard's voice was back to normal, if disturbingly quiet.

'At my behest. It was my intention to tell you after your meeting in Paris. If Janssens and Rossignol had reached agreement then I would have had to move quickly. But they didn't and don't look like doing so.'

'So you think that justifies what you've done?'

'We are Ashworth's advisers. If Ashworth's asked us to approach Hitler, Mussolini and Roosevelt separately and secretly on their behalf we'd do it. You know that.'

'But we'd tell each other, wouldn't we? We are on the same side, aren't we?'

Jeremy shifted a little. 'You were acting with Maucourt's.

They do not act for Ashworth's. They're Malfait's crowd.'

His uncle closed his eyes. 'Maucourt's and White's are colleagues. I am a director of Maucourt's and I am a White!' He slammed his hand down on the table. 'Damn it, Jeremy, you can't go on acting in this insular manner! The whole point of our alliance with Maucourt Frères is nullified by your attitude. We have got to behave in unison.' His eyes travelled back to me. 'I believed that we were acting in unison. Janssens' call came as a complete shock to me. Why didn't you warn me?'

I shook my head in self-reproach. 'I'm afraid I went off on a trail to Lens, Richard. I didn't think Janssens would do that. I didn't think he'd try to act the outraged innocent; that never occurred to me.'

'Why not?'

I braced myself to impart disturbing information.

'Because I believe he's stolen Pierre Martens' work, he's probably responsible for his murder, and he and one of Malfait's managers, François Kolewski, are sharing a common mistress: Janssen's blonde Marketing chief, Eliza-beth van Laeten.'

That made them forget their differences. There was a shocked silence. Then they both clamoured at me until I calmed them down. They stayed silent while I told them everything that I'd seen on my trek round Roubaix and Tourcoing, and of my suspicions, and of my conversations with Kolewski and the Ashworths. I also told them I had no proper evidence, so there was no point in going to the police. Only forensic results, and there didn't seem to be much of those, could positively incriminate anybody. That was why I'd stirred Janssens up.

But of the liaison between Kolewski and Elizabeth van Laeten I had no doubt.

'The only chance,' I said, shortly, 'is if Janssens is too eager with the computer work and makes it obvious he's using something unique to Martens. From what Philip Ashworth says that's unlikely because any good logical approach will go the same way as Martens. What Janssens will gain is time, valuable time, and a lot of development experimentation. If I am right, that is.'

Jeremy looked gloomily at his desktop. 'It sounds horribly logical, Tim. My God, these Continental things are complicated. What a triangle! It virtually ensures that Martens' information has flowed from Kolewski via this van Laeten woman to Janssens. No wonder he's offering only a rock-bottom price. And if he gets Rossignol, the computer work will be his anyway, so no one will detect its theft. The Ashworths are well out of the whole mess.'

'Malfait won't sell at that price.' Sir Richard was back to a crisp tone. 'Eugène Maucourt would oppose it, too.'

Jeremy pursed his lips. 'He might, Richard. I hear that Malfait is often short of cash. He may decide to cut his losses, or deal the thing in return for some other ministerial favour. A promise—worthless of course—from Janssens to keep Rossignol going would keep him sweet with his authorities.'

'Ashworth's could still drop the Janssens side and combine with Rossignol.' Sir Richard was getting dogged. 'There could be synergy there.'

I shook my head. 'It's not a match, Richard. Janssens is the key to this triangle and he's put himself in a very powerful position. The only chance is—well, no, it's not, really—'

'What?'

I put my hands in my pockets. 'Kolewski. His position is ambiguous. He obviously hates Malfait and I think has acted in what he sees as his own interests towards Janssens. But the Elizabeth van Laeten connection is very dangerous. I don't know what Janssens may have promised him in return for what I think he's done, or how far he's committed himself, but I could sound him out. He seems to trust me.

Surely he must be worried about the relationships? And I've deliberately rattled Janssens. It could lead to something.'

Sir Richard shook his head vigorously. 'I don't think so. I don't think there is any role for the Bank to play now, as far as the Janssens side of the thing is concerned. Nor to dig into possible murder and theft. Such things are for the police. We have no business to interfere.'

'I quite agree.' Jeremy was as emphatic as his uncle. 'Stay out of it, Tim. Better to let the thing go than to get involved in any clever shenanigans. It's too risky. I know you hate leaving stones unturned but without hard proof you'll only cause terrible trouble.'

I sighed. I'd been hoping not to give them the whole pattern of things as I saw it, trying to keep from setting it out until I'd had more time to dig up some facts. Somewhere in that flat expanse of cockpit country on the western edge of Belgium and the north-east corner of France there lay information that would settle my mind. But if they were going to issue edicts to keep me out of things I was going to be unhappy; I couldn't leave things unfinished. I simply couldn't. So that's why I sighed before I spoke. I knew that when I spoke I'd raise all their ingrained prejudices about matters connected with the Art Fund, and me, and violent occurrences.

'It's a bit more complicated than just avoiding Kolewski,' I said. 'Quite a bit more complicated than that. I can't just leave it at that.'

'Why not?' Jeremy frowned at me.

'Well . . .' I hesitated because I was coming to the hard part. 'In a way, I think it has to do with a painting, you see. And a book.'

'A painting?' Horror suffused his voice. 'What painting? You've never mentioned a painting up to now.'

'No.' I managed to meet his shocked expression, knowing there was going to be a big problem convincing them both that I should carry on, but carry on I must. 'It's just, well, it's just in a way, you see. A connection. It's a painting Philip Ashworth would like me to buy. A war painting, First World War that is, by a man called Nevinson. Don't look so shell-shocked, Jeremy. Think about it: there's always been a painting in these things somewhere, hasn't there?'

'Too true there has! If there are going to be paintings involved I'm damn sure you should stay out of it. Everything tells me to run, and run like hell!' Jeremy's expression suddenly changed and became indignant. 'To think you called me duplicitous! When we had lunch together you swore blind that there were no paintings in prospect.'

Sir Richard was staring at me in almost rigid fascination. He didn't seem to have heard Jeremy, or to be interested in paintings at all. 'A book? What book?'

I looked him back, straight in the eye. 'It's a book which provides the Janssens connection. Remember our first morning, at Cuinchy? It's a first edition of one of Robert Graves's volumes of poetry. From 1917. *Fairies and Fusiliers*, it's called.'

18

The town of Roeselare is not particularly noted as either a tourist spot or for its prowess as a cultural centre. It used to be a pretty villainous small market town you had to grind through if you wanted to go from Lille to Ostend, although why you'd want to do that is debatable. The A17 autoroute from Courtrai and Lille bypasses the town for you now or you can circle the place on the older N36 which cuts west just above a place called Passchendaele, which you may have heard of on account of its mud in 1917. Nevinson was one of the very few artists to paint there.

The countryside is flat, damp and depressing. It was so badly drained in 1917 that the trenches filled with water and the guns churned up a lethal quagmire. Modern prosperity has domesticated the farmland into green, carefully-cultivated squares among the ploughed bits and smartened up the town's market square but it's still no Bruges. The places to the west carry their evocative and tragic names among little canals and flat waterlands—it's not called the Low Countries for nothing—but I veered off the western bypass so as to get in to the Town Hall and start my searches among the cobbles and incipient mud. Cold rain drizzled on to the market stalls. It was going to be difficult, I thought, not speaking Flemish and wanting to dig up old graves, so to speak. I'm not sure how the local authorities in Britain react to foreign investigators who are neither family nor authorized but I could imagine they might be difficult, so in a traditionally taciturn part of Belgium I might have a severe problem.

I concocted a cover story of the renewal of old wartime ties for a relative now too aged to do his own research and took the plunge. I was entirely wrong about everything; they were helpful and the secretary at the Town Hall spoke almost perfect English.

I was there and in the environs of Roeselare nearly all day. I could have spent much longer if I hadn't needed to concentrate on the job in hand, because history presses in on you all the time in that area. Just about everyone has tramped and fought their way across it, thinking every time that they were unique and it would never happen this way again. It always has. Nearly fifty years of peace, no matter how uneasy, has settled things to a calm that everyone assumes to be permanent but battles are still there to be fought, even if only on a tiny scale now, in little lethal bursts and skirmishes.

It was quite late when I finished. In a sense I dallied too long, but it was a displacement activity, a thing to occupy me while I avoided going to do what I knew had now become a necessity. Even the way I got back into my car was reluctant.

The price you pay for not being bored is the size of the risk you're prepared to take.

In the dark I drove slowly, pondering my way back towards Courtrai, then veered off to Tourcoing, low and dark brick on either side of tramlined and sometimes still-cobbled streets. Not far from the brasserie where I'd seen François Kolewski and Elizabeth van Laeten, I parked and walked in the chill drizzle until the bright lights drew me in for a beer.

The place was warm and cheerful. I stood at the bar like four or five other men, sipping cautiously and running my eye over the tables where people were starting to eat.

'Tell me,' I asked the barman, when things were quiet, 'is Mr Kolewski coming in tonight?'

He looked blank. 'Who?'

'Kolewski. Big fellow. Couldn't miss him. Used to play rugby for Lille. Face like a mashed potato.'

He shook his head. 'Not familiar to me. Hang on; I'll ask the head waiter.'

I took a deeper swig of beer. Kolewski would hardly eat here without doing what I was doing first. The barman was standing by the kitchen door talking to a waiter, an older man, dressed in black. Neither of them glanced in my direction. Outside the rain was becoming more persistent, increasing in density. It wasn't a night to go out in unless you headed for a hostelry like this.

'Sorry.' The barman was back in front of me. 'No one like that we know of. No reservations, either.'

'You mean you don't know him?'

He shook his head.

'I could have sworn he comes here regularly. With a blonde lady. Slim, very attractive.'

'No. Sorry. Don't remember anyone like that.'

'Oh well, I must have got it wrong. Thanks all the same.'

The barman eyed me curiously. 'English?'

'Yes, I'm English.'

'Rugby?'

'In the old days.'

The barman grimaced. He didn't say anything offensive about referees and foul play because he didn't need to. The last four matches between England and France were something that Frenchmen would rather forget.

It was a cold trail, though. No proof of a connection between Kolewski and Elizabeth van Laeten would be forthcoming here. So far I had only myself as company or witness.

I finished the beer and went back to my car. It took about twenty minutes to negotiate my way into Roubaix and find the Rue de la Perche once again. No. 19 was in darkness, exactly as before. I parked across the street and sat in the dark, falling rain trickling over the car surfaces, dappling the windscreen. Kolewski might be in Le Café des Sports, quaffing at his local, but somehow I didn't think so. Even if he were, I didn't want to meet him there. I needed to see him alone now, not with Elizabeth van Laeten or anyone else. I was having trouble getting everything sorted out in my head. Half the time I sat there I spent sorting, and half twitching nervously whenever a car came down the Rue de la Perche, in case it was him. Either way I wasn't getting my thinking nearly as clear as I'd have liked.

It was four o'clock when he showed up. His car turned into the street at the top, where the main road lighting seemed subdued, and came carefully along until it parked outside his front door. I've never felt worse. I was stiff and cold and fearful, bug-eyed with staring out through the dappled windscreen in case I missed him, gritty in the joints from sitting out a long black night. When I moved to open my car door as quietly as possible I could have sworn I heard a creak from my knees. Somehow, though, I did manage to move quietly and quickly, so that I was right behind him as he put his key into his front door.

'François?'

He nearly jumped out of his skin. His big frame twisted sideways and he went as stiff as iron. Half-turned, tense, one fist bunched, the other still holding the key in the front door, he confronted me. His ugly features were creased with suspicion.

'Sorry to give you a fright. I've been waiting for you.'

He didn't answer. He didn't say hello Tim, slap my back, demand to know what on earth I was doing there, at that time. He just stared blackly back at me, waiting for an explanation. In his eyes I saw a glint of hostility reflected from a dim side-street lamp. Things didn't look good.

'It's late, I know. Can I come in? You are alone, aren't you?'

He nodded once, briefly. In answer to both questions or one, he didn't clarify. He turned back to the door, glanced up and down the street, opened up and went in without a word. I followed into a narrow entrance passage. A light clicked on and I found myself staring at his great shaggy back, encased in the bear-like coat.

We went down the passage into a back room with a small kitchen off it. A smell of damp uncleanliness mustily blocked my nostrils. There was a window, tight shut, with shutters drawn. A bachelor pad, with a messy table sporting used crockery, cutlery, and half a French loaf gone stale. Empty wine and beer bottles stood on a side dresser with linoleum-covered shelves. He probably ate breakfast here but not much else; I didn't see him as a home-cookery man.

He walked round the other side of the table, shrugged off his huge coat, picked up an empty wine bottle, put it down and stared across the litter at me. I left my own Crombie on—the house didn't seem to be heated—and looked back at him.

'Well?' he demanded. There was no hint of beery bonhomie now. 'What do you want?'

'Janssens pulled out. It looks as though Malfait has to find another buyer.'

He scowled. 'I know that. Not much you did for Roubaix at that Paris meeting. So what? You haven't come here now, at this hour, to tell me that.'

'No, I haven't, that's true.' I put my hands in my overcoat pockets. 'I wanted to talk to you before I jumped to conclusions. I owe you that. For the sake of old times and absent friends.'

'Conclusions? What conclusions?'

'About how Janssens got hold of Martens' computer research. And why Martens was murdered.'

'Murdered? What do you mean?'

'I think he was murdered. I think it's too much of a coincidence that everyone else got out but not Pierre Martens. I think he was knocked down in the raw material store and then the fire was started there deliberately. To wipe him out.'

His battered mouth twitched. His eyes narrowed at me. 'How do you come to believe that?'

'Because I'm sure that Janssens has got all the information he needs. And he's very confident. If he weren't so confident he wouldn't be making official protests to my boss. He'd be trying to wipe me out. Probably using you.'

'Me?'

'Yes. You. You were the liaison man between Roubaix and Wingles. You had all Martens' material. And you were there when the fire started. I think you've passed him all that material.'

His eyes met mine. Tension was starting to build in his body; he was moving on to the balls of his feet.

'I think there are two explanations of why Martens was murdered. I'm not sure which is the right one.'

'Oh?' Slightly more forward, his body tilted into a poise.

'Yes. I think that he found out you were passing his material on to Janssens. He threatened to expose the whole thing, in fact he was on the point of exposing it, when you caught him unawares. Put a match to the factory and to him, after you'd laid him out cold in the raw material store. While no one was looking. Janssens is so convinced that the evidence is impossible to establish that he's acting very confidently, even though it must have been touch and go at the time, because Martens was late into work. And you disappeared very smartly after the fire. I wondered why I didn't meet you then. I imagine you had evidence to get rid of?'

'Do you really?'

'Oh yes. Whether it was a rabbit skin or something else, you could have had traces of petrol or something on you. But Janssens is right to be confident. No one seems to have a shred of tangible evidence of what I've been saying.'

'Ah.' A slight relaxation was detachable. 'And what is your other explanation?'

'Oh, that I think that it's possible Martens not only found out about your thieving his material but he also saw you and Elizabeth van Laeten together somewhere. Who knows? Lille, or Lens, or Ostend, or Paris. Anywhere. Your passion for her made you careless, perhaps.'

He had frozen again, gone back into terrible tension. I was looking at sudden death any second now.

'To start with she was just your line of contact. So you and Janssens wouldn't be seen together. Once you started going to bed with her the situation was very different. Martens was a double danger to you. You've come from her now, I expect. Unfortunately, I saw you together as well. In Tourcoing. By a brasserie called—'

He shoved the table from the top edge with the force of a battering ram. I had my hands out of my overcoat pockets at his first flick of movement, like a gunfighter in a Western on the draw, but the table rammed into my thighs, crockery flying and cutlery scattering, to pin me to a sideboard like a leg-vice. Then, with his full weight leaning against the table, he reached across with two enormous arms to grab my throat in his ham-like fists.

My first reaction was to catch his arms, to try and prise the throttle off my throat, but that was a mistake. His arms were stronger, and longer than mine. But to hold my throat he had to bend those arms in a grip, bringing his head close enough for me to jab him in both eyes with my thumbs. For a moment he stood it and we were locked like that, me going into a black dizzy pressure as my lungs started to burst and my head sang, he feeling my thumbnails going

deeper into his eyes as he throttled but pushed back. Then
he broke to grab at my hands and, as I kept them clear of
his crushing fists, I rammed the table back at him to give
myself a little space.

Slightly off balance, he moved back just an inch or two,
which was enough. I jumped out from behind the table as
the gap widened that inch and was at its side, lashing a
blow to his head to connect behind the ear. Then we were
at it, hitting and grappling all over the room, bottles flying,
cups smashed, me doing enough to keep him at bay—my
blood was up and I got two really good punches to his
face despite feeling strangled—but knowing him to be the
stronger, bigger man with as many tricks up his sleeve as
I had. My head-on strategy had worked far too well.

Balked of strangling me, he ignored my bruised neck and
snatched a bread knife off the desecrated table, where it
had come to rest with the stale half-loaf against a broken
jug. It had a standard serrated blade about eight inches
long, a thing with a wooden handle, the most common
domestic murder weapon in the world. The sight of it filled
me with both dread and relief. Relief because a straight
physical contest favoured him; dread because getting skew-
ered with a serrated bread knife is not the way I'd choose
to go, not any time, and he was likely to be very dangerous
with it.

He held it first like a sword, blade pointing at me, ready
for a lunge. With his strength he was banking on pushing
the thing into me against all opposition and his heave forward was bunched behind the blade with all his might. I
dodged sideways so that the knife missed, grabbed his arm
and locked my right leg between his. For a few seconds we
stood like that, muscles straining, heaving for leverage,
teeth bared, his arm stuck straight out as I'd clamped it,
knife pointing at the wall. Then I felt rather than saw his
fingers squiggle as he jiggled the knife round to re-grasp it,

blade down in his bunched fist in preparation for a down-ward push at my chest.

Slowly, both of us gasping with effort, sweat starting to stream, he brought the arm over and up to poise the knife above me. My overcoat was thick but with his strength it would be no protection against the driving force he'd put behind the point. It came, bit by bit, closer to me, and closer. Both of us were concentrating like mad on that one final action, that deciding issue, when I broke my right leg clamp to ram my knee behind his and made a terrific heave, scrimmage-style, to swing him over. We went down to the floor together in a mad tight embrace, me still clamping his knife wrist hard to turn it away with all the strength I'd got. The crash as we hit the ground came from what was left on the table dancing with the impact.

He let out a sort of strangled roar. His muscles slackened. His eyes, close to mine, widened, then seemed to jam open wide. There on the floor, side by side in the litter, the balance of our embrace changed. My side was still tense; his was a stiff, heavy inertia. His arm wasn't trying to push the knife into me any more. Looking down, I could see my hand still clamping his wrist and his fingers round the wooden handle of the knife, with the blade under him somewhere.

His mouth moved in a hoarse whisper.

'*Merde!*'

'François?'

He didn't answer. I let go of the wrist. The wooden handle stuck outwards from under his jacket with a fixity that I didn't like.

'François?'

My Crombie had something liquid on it. I disengaged from him awkwardly, still fearful of a trick, and, untangling myself, scrambled to my feet. I looked down, and suddenly saw that there was a thick smear of blood on my fingers.

Kolewski gave a sort of twitch, his huge frame moving erratically once or twice, his eyes still staring wide, half at me, half into the distance. Then he went very still. The open eyes seemed to droop. His left leg, after the stillness, moved outwards slowly and back, knee bent, stopping when it touched his other leg. His head lowered to the floor reluctantly, as though the muscles wanted to stop it.

I bent down and felt his pulse.

At first I thought it was feeble, but then I realized my own was thundering like a rhino's, so I took a deep breath and tried again.

There wasn't one.

I leant up against the table and shook for a bit. Then I managed to move off and rinsed my hands under the tap in the kitchen. The smell of damp mustiness came back strongly from my overpressured, blood-filled nostrils, giving me the willies. I practically ran down the narrow passage and out of the front door into the steady rain, slamming the door after me and breathing the cold wet air with panicky relief. The car started first turn of the key. I drove out of the Rue de la Perche in Roubaix with the fervour of a man who never wishes to see the Rue de la Perche in Roubaix again, never, not at any time in his life, not for a million pounds. In less than fifteen minutes I was back in Belgium and fifteen later I was entering the south side of Courtrai.

Pulling into a side turning, I stopped and started to get my breath back. There'd be time enough for me to report Kolewski's death as the sun rose; grey light was clarifying the route ahead already. My obsession was with Janssens now, Bob Janssens, and his father Louis, and the cockpit country I'd spent the day in yesterday. Was it only yesterday? I needed to get into that smooth modern office before Janssens did, or at least at the same time as him, and look in the ridiculously bombé bureau bookcase. Otherwise everything was for nothing.

After a while I summoned up courage, drove to the factory and parked in front of the three flagpoles, by the evergreen garden. The Janssens factory worked shifts and as I got out of the car I could hear the distant hum of factory activity. A sleepy nightwatchman sat in the foyer behind a reception desk, looking at a grey, flickering television screen.

My luck was in; the glass front door wasn't locked.

'Mr Janssens' office,' I barked at the nightwatchman as I half-ran past. 'I'm going to Mr Janssens' office. It's an emergency.'

'Hey! Wait!'

I went up to the first floor three stairs at a time, through the secretary's ante-room and into the smart office, with its bordered carpet, its moulded chairs and the big bureau bookcase bulging on one wall. The glazed doors of the bookcase opened first wrench and I thumbed past the popular edition of Penguin poets to look for the first edition I'd seen before.

It wasn't there.

Fairies and Fusiliers by Robert Graves. Published by Heinemann, 1917.

It wasn't there. I searched up and down the spines of the other books, then I stood rigid, staring at them as boots squelched rapidly up the staircase towards the offices.

It had gone.

The nightwatchman had collected another security man to bring with him. They came into the office quickly in their black uniforms and stood in the doorway for one moment, cautiously, to look at me as people might look at a madman or a dangerous, escaped animal from a zoo. I closed the glazed doors. It had gone; the slim volume had gone. Everything was going wrong.

Perhaps it had been hidden deliberately?

'It's all right,' I said to the two broad Flemish faces

staring at me. 'I'll explain to Mr Janssens. Either here or at his home. When he comes in to work, perhaps. I need to see him urgently.' Suddenly I felt tired; where could I look now? A showdown with Janssens—again—was becoming a necessity.

The second security man stared at me more intently, a broad Flemish stare from a big-boned Flemish man.

'Mr Janssens is dead, monsieur,' he said stolidly. He said it with reproof in his voice, as though I had desecrated something.

It took me a good ten seconds to take in what he'd said. *'Dead?'*

The security man nodded, without expression.

'He was found dead in his car, in the early hours of this morning. Near Oudenaarde.'

'Dead?'

'He was strangled, we have been told. These offices are under strict surveillance. There is blood on your coat, monsieur. Please stay exactly where you are. The police will be here very shortly.'

19

The police inspector in charge of the case was called Claessens. He was a small, dark, fairly plump Belgian in a three-piece suit with a waistcoat that fitted much too tightly. Creases corrugated his buttoned stomach. On the whole he was grave but not unfriendly and his station's coffee was pretty good; strong but not bitter or overstewed. He and his sergeants listened to the story I told them several times before it was all written down and typed. Then I signed it. They went away and left me to be watched for quite a long time while nothing much seemed to happen.

If I were a smoker I'd have smoked a lot.

'It's always difficult,' the policeman watching me said gloomily, 'when it's an affair with French complications. Official channels, and all that. You wouldn't think, in 1992, that things were still so nationalistic.'

No one had explained what took Janssens to Oudenaarde. When I was at school you had to learn all those battles of Marlborough's; Oudenaarde, Malplaquet, the lot. It would be a cross-country way to go to Brussels, if that was where Janssens was headed. Claessens was terse about details. They took my Crombie away as though they might find traces of Janssens on it, and gave me a receipt. They took swabs from my hands and carried off my shoes. After a while they gave me a hamburger and chips, with more coffee. That must have been about lunch-time. I fell asleep after eating it and was woken by Claessens returning with one of his sergeants, complete with notebook. They didn't start the tape-recorder in the interview room and I'm not sure what time it was.

'I think you should know,' Claessens said severely, 'that

the van Laeten family is highly respected in Kortrijk.'

He pronounced Courtrai in the Flemish way—Kortrijk
—so you'd be quite sure where his sympathies lay.

'I'm sure they are,' I said, respectfully, thinking that it
happens in the best of families, but I'd better not say that.

'Miss Elizabeth van Laeten denies absolutely that there
was anything untoward, any impropriety, in her relations
with the late Mr Janssens. And as for this Kolewski, she
was shocked at the suggestion you have made. She denies
any relationship—commercial or otherwise—with him.'

'Well,' I said, using the famous response, 'she would,
wouldn't she?'

'You state yourself that to your knowledge you are the
only person to have seen Kolewski and van Laeten together?'

'To my knowledge, yes.'

'And this brasserie in Tourcoing could not link them,
either?'

'It seems not.'

'Then your statement will be difficult to corroborate, Mr
Simpson.'

That started to make me irritable. Unshaven, I am irritable anyway. With a sore neck I am much worse.

'Oh, come on, Inspector, do try a little. A senior businessman has been murdered. Kolewski had both motive and
opportunity. You can examine the Janssens business for
evidence of Martens' work—disks, documents and so on—
and you can carry out forensic examination of Janssens',
Kolewski's and van Laeten's cars for evidence of the presence of any of them in each other's vehicles. Kolewski had
a most distinctive coat. Fibres should be identifiable. I have
to mention that he changed it when he met Elizabeth van
Laeten but the change overcoat will be identifiable, too.'

He ignored my suggestions. 'Why do you say Kolewski
had motive?'

'Jealousy, for one thing. Or commercially, perhaps. He and Janssens may have fallen out over remuneration. Or Janssens may have found out about van Laeten and told Kolewski to sling his hook, to clear out. Perhaps they had a violent row about it. Perhaps he wouldn't pay up or employ Kolewski as he may have promised. Kolewski tried to strangle me, as I've told you. You can see my neck; it's bloody sore. You say Janssens was strangled, so there you are.'

'Mr Janssens was not strangled with bare hands. He was strangled with his own scarf. We think, I must say, that he knew his attacker. He agreed to meet him, or her, in a quiet roadside place outside Oudenaarde. His presence there is otherwise inexplicable.' He stared at me meaningfully. 'You knew Mr Janssens. He might have gone to meet you.'

'Well, he didn't. I went to the brasserie in Tourcoing and then I waited outside Kolewski's house. I didn't have any reason to kill Janssens. Or Martens. And scarf or hands, Kolewski was a strangler.'

'As no doubt you will explain to the French police when they arrest you.'

'Eh?'

'When they arrest you. We will be taking you to the border to hand you over shortly. You have, after all, admitted killing Kolewski, even though you claim self-defence. I do not have grounds for thinking that you killed Mr Janssens and the French are anxious to question you. I can always get you back again if need be.'

'Shuttlecock and battledore.'

'I beg your pardon?'

'Just an expression.'

Claessens stared at me for a while, then said, almost out of the blue, 'You have not explained why, when you were detained, you were looking in the bureau bookcase in Janssens' office. The security men were quite specific on that point. Your behaviour was odd, they said. No one bulldozes past security men just to look in a bookcase. Not usually.'

'Oh yes I have told you. I was looking for evidence of Martens' material. Disks, documents and so on.'

'Ah. Quite so. You did say that.' Claessens eyes were on mine as he nodded. 'Surely you do not think, however, that Janssens would place incriminating material in so obvious a spot?'

'You never can tell. There was a great detective who said that the obvious place is often the best.'

Claessens' Belgian expression became alert, defensive. 'Which great detective?'

'Oh, I don't know. Sherlock Holmes, probably.'

His expression relaxed and became slightly humorous. 'Ah. Possibly. I think it was Auguste Dupin, actually. Nevertheless, it seems unlikely that you would have found the material there. Janssens was a sophisticated, a very intelligent man.'

He stared at me again. You English, the stare said, you seem so ingenuous sometimes, but can you really be? What are you hiding from me?

I looked back at him as innocently as I could. He wouldn't have believed what I told him, anyway.

That's how I justify not having told him; in reality, I just didn't want to.

I kept my face straight. 'I'm afraid I didn't like him, Inspector. My dislike was not enough to turn to murder, but I think he behaved criminally. Using Kolewski for the dirty work.'

Claessens grunted. 'We will see. It is time to take you to France. I think we will be in contact again soon, Mr Simpson.'

'A pleasure, I'm sure.'

He grinned suddenly. 'You're a cool fellow. Very cool.'

'Thank you. I take that, from a Fleming, as a real compliment.'

We parted with some courtesy. They took me in a van, all of forty minutes or so, to Tourcoing, and in no time I was in a French police station, with a French police inspector and sergeant, sitting in front of me, filling in forms. I made the same set of statements, had my fingerprints taken, saw my overcoat being carried in a transparent plastic bag like a dry cleaner's, had a small black coffee, ate a sandwich.

I had plenty of time to rub my face with my hands, scratch my head, and think back over the events which had brought me to this closely-guarded condition.

Thus it must be with a life of crime.

The French inspector was called Aumage. Inspector Aumage.

'You first met Kolewski on a rugby tour?'

'That's it.'

'You played for England?'

'Good heavens, no. Not that level. I played for my University. We toured with scratch sides. You know: friendly matches.'

He gave me a look. 'Friendly matches? Then you killed him?'

'Oh, come on, Inspector. It wasn't the Parc des Princes, you know.'

He had the decency to smile. 'But it was quite a coincidence, eh? Coming across him after all those years.'

'The world is full of ex-rugger players, Inspector. We're quite a clan. And I hadn't known him well. He sought me out; probably to check whether I was likely to be a danger.'

'Why did he attack you?'

'If he'd just come from Oudenaarde, he must have been in quite a state. I could link him to Elizabeth van Laeten. Everything else was just theory. An affair with Janssens' marketing director was something which, if corroborated, would put a different complexion on things. I believe that if Claessens and the Belgian police apply the necessary pressure, and do the forensic work, the truth will come out.'

He let his face go back to a blank. 'Possibly. Patience will be needed, Mr Simpson. And in the meantime there is your admission that you killed Kolewski, fled the country, and were arrested in Janssens' office in Courtrai. You may make a telephone call if you wish, but you will stay here.'

For supper they served me a hamburger and chips; the gastronomic border was imperceptible. My call to Maucourt Frères would cause considerable activity but my part now was to try and be patient. I slept quite well considering that the light stayed on all night and in the morning I was allowed to shave with a French disposable razor. I think I probably looked quite respectable, despite borrowed shoes, when Inspector Aumage called me to an interview room, at about mid-day.

'There are not one, but four people here to see you,' he said. 'And I have received a copy of your dossier, from Paris.'

'Dossier? Me? Paris?'

He gave me an old-fashioned look. 'The record of your dealings with Inspector Dagallier in Meudon and Inspector Levroux of the *Huitième Arrondissement* last year are all recorded here.' He tapped a file in front of him. 'It seems you have a reputation to consider.'

'A reputation?'

'You have been remarkably cool. Claessens has made an observation on it. But I see from these papers that you have killed a man before. Two men. Possibly more. In self-defence as well, it was alleged.'

'It was in self-defence, let me tell you. It certainly was.'

'And you are in the habit of placing yourself in a position where killing other men in self-defence is a regular occurrence?'

'Certainly not.'

Aumage's mouth twitched. 'As I think your playwright Wilde observed, once is allowable but twice is just plain careless, Mr Simpson.'

'Actually, Lady Bracknell says that once is a misfortune, twice looks like carelessness. She makes the remark about the ability to lose parents, rather than what you have in mind. Pierre Martens might have agreed, however.'

He grinned, then straightened his face. 'The examining magistrate has seen the papers. The bruises on your neck do tally with the version you have given us. Claessens advises that Janssens received a call, late last night, which caused him to go to his office and then depart for an unknown destination. Presumably Oudenaarde. Neither he nor I can understand why that place was chosen, but so far there is nothing to link you with it, nor any motive that suffices to hold you. However, your car, which has been impounded by Claessens' men, is being carefully searched for forensic evidence. You will be allowed to see two of your visitors—one is the lawyer from the Maucourt bank—here now. It seems that the required guarantees can be arranged to enable your release to be effected. The lawyer has the necessary documents for signature and will doubtless explain them to you. You'll have to come back here, and to Belgium, when needed.' The old-fashioned look returned. 'We can always get you back if need be. You are fortunate to be released so quickly. Not everyone has such influential friends.'

'Oh?'

Inspector Aumage smiled again, slightly. 'Mr Jean Malfait? The great industrialist? In person? You are indeed honoured, Mr Simpson.' He stood up. 'I'll let them in, now.'

The lawyer from Maucourt's was familiar; he gave me a deferential smile—I was probably earning him a lot of money—and many papers to sign. The man with him was Malfait. After shaking hands, he waved grandly at the lawyer and told me to keep signing while he talked. He leaned towards me genially as I scribbled signatures.

'We must get you out of here as quickly as possible,' he said. He smelled of very expensive after-shave. 'Rossignol owes you a hefty debt, Mr Simpson. It is the least we can do.'

'Oh?'

'Of course. I did not suspect that one of my own managers would be stealing Martens' research on behalf of a competitor. You have uncovered something which explains a lot.' He sighed grandly. 'Human greed must never be underestimated. I have no doubt that the necessary evidence will come to light.'

'I certainly hope so.' I didn't think it was the moment to suggest to him that Kolewski might have been motivated by anxiety as much as greed. Or that he believed that the Roubaix factory was threatened and was worried about Malfait's intentions, possibly even hated him.

'It will.' His face moved into a hard expression. 'If the police don't find the evidence, I certainly will. Have no doubt of that. I am in your debt and you have behaved with courage.' His look held mine directly. 'If ever you are in need of help, or occupation, please do not hesitate to contact me. With my activities there is always a place for a man like you.'

'That's very kind. I'm most grateful to you for getting me out of here so quickly.' I was; I didn't fancy another night in gaol, not even close to so civilized a cop as Inspector Aumage.

Malfait waved a hand in a dismissive gesture. 'Merely a formality. The least I could do. And I have always got business to attend to round here.'

The lawyer bustled out and came back a few minutes

later. The doors opened. You sign papers, make financial
guarantees, undertake to meet obligations. People step
aside, even bow.

Thus it must be with a successful business life.

The other two waiting for me were Eugène Maucourt
and Sir Richard White. Maucourt, for him, was quite effu-
sive. Sir Richard looked at me anxiously.

'Are you all right? We're taking you back to Paris.'

'Not too bad. Can we leave right away?'

'Of course.' He kept the anxious stare and said no words
of reproach.

Malfait and the lawyer shook hands and departed to their
expensive activities. Eugène Maucourt got into the front of
a chauffeur-driven limousine and Sir Richard and I got into
the back. We pulled away quickly and Eugène Maucourt
spoke up.

'I hope your experiences have not upset you too much,
Mr Simpson.' He twisted round to look at me. 'Or may I
call you Tim? After all, we know each other well now, don't
we?'

'It's fine by me.'

'OK. I am glad. You should know that Malfait is very
pleased. I'm sure he's told you. He has alternative strategies
for Rossignol now anyway—the Janssens rejection stirred
him to make other approaches to French carpet manufacturers which Charville, good fellow, has suggested—and he
has asked us to assist in implementing those strategies.
Excellent for us.'

'Good.'

So much, I thought privately, for that grandiose meeting
in the formal room off the Rue du Faubourg Saint-Honoré,
the eloquence about the restructuring of the carpet industry, a revolutionary new computer facility of the highest
order, trans-European groupings and stiff competition for
Beaulieu Tufting. In practice it comes down to arson, mur-

der, theft, passion and grubbing back to other national
companies to build a life-raft in one's own country. An
integrated Europe is going to take time.

'He has asked if we will retain you as adviser to our team.
He particularly wishes to involve you.' Maucourt managed
to smile quite warmly. 'He feels that your combination of
business experience, investigative flair and, er, courageous
approach are most valuable assets. For myself, I would be
glad if Maucourt Frères and White's could work more
closely not just at a senior but also at an, er, an operating
level.'

'I'm sure that's desirable.'

Sir Richard gave me a knowing look. His attitude was
still anxious and I caught him watching my expression
intently.

'You sure you're all right? They treated you well?'

'I'm OK, Richard. I need a bath.' I stared out of the
window. We were drawing away from Lille on the A1 Paris
motorway and I saw the sign for the Lens exit coming up
ahead. 'Would you mind if we made one stop? I'd like to
go back to the site at Cuinchy, where we first met. Off the
road from La Bassée to Cambrin and Béthune. It's not far
out of our way. Just to sort my mind out?'

'Of course.' Sir Richard gave instructions to the driver.
We missed the centre of Wingles this time, but we went
through Auchy and were soon over the canal and alongside
the field where, not so many days before, he and Janssens
and Jack Ashworth and I had met.

I clambered out of the car and stretched my legs. Eugène
Maucourt and Sir Richard got out to follow me. The winter
crop had progressed half an inch or so further and greenness
was spreading across the countryside. In the distance the
spire of La Bassée glinted as the afternoon sun briefly got
through a gap in the wet clouds. The air was keen and fresh;
the field in which Robert Graves was muddily entrenched to

face the Germans looked productive and carefully farmed.

'It was a delaying tactic, you know,' I said to Sir Richard. 'Martens delayed his arrival at work because he went to the post office in Lens to send a special letter or packet to someone. We'll never know who. And he was hoping to meet you later. But Janssens and Kolewski had already decided to do him in. It must have been quite a panic. This was the nearest historic site to Wingles that Janssens could think of so he got us to come here. He was a Graves fan. Ever since he was small, I imagine. As I told you and Jeremy, his father had Graves's work in his office and he must have picked it up young. So he brought us here, for long enough to let Kolewski do his work.'

Sir Richard's face twisted. 'Grisly. I thought he was genuinely showing me this out of kindness. What a bastard.'

'Yes.'

'Well, he met the right fate, anyway. Done in by his own assassin. Who you—'

He stopped and gave me a cautious stare. I didn't react to it. Eugène Maucourt was looking up the road towards Festubert, where the Guards have a cemetery, and the chauffeur was dusting the bonnet of the car. Round us the countryside went on about its business, with a tractor growling along behind us and a distant buzz of traffic murmuring from the main road between La Bassée and Cambrin. The poetry that Graves wrote about this little piece of ground, the glinting spire of La Bassée looking down on death after death, is inked black on pages which must now open less and less frequently. It was an odd quirk of criminal invention to have brought us here, to have reminded me of Graves's spellbinding book while Pierre Martens lay cremating in an inferno of white-hot polyurethane foam. The place, now, bore no sign of any mortal events, no trace of its past and recent horrors. Nothing might have happened here at all.

'It was a delaying tactic,' I repeated. 'In more ways than one.'

'Why?'

'It delayed our arrival at Wingles. And, quite incidentally, it had me concentrating, for most of the time, on the wrong war.'

He raised his eyebrows at me in query, but a gust of cold spring breeze coming across the fields from Cuinchy made me shiver and I gestured at the car.

'Come on, that's enough. Let's get on our way. I have only one more slight deviation to request. It's not out of our way. We can join the A1 autoroute further south.'

'Why? What's that?'

I looked across the field and thought of machine-guns dealing out their dotted message of death. A mental image of a long desolate track going over devastated rolling country, seen printed in books but last viewed on a video screen in Sue's company at the Imperial War Museum, had come to mind, was occupying it irresistibly.

I have this thing about being there, about visiting the site.

'I would like,' I said, 'to drive down the road from Arras to Bapaume.'

20

Christopher Richard Wynne Nevinson must have come very close to persuading himself that he was not a failure. He had a talent for widespread publicity and he contributed articles to newspapers, on all kinds of subjects, prolifically. He gave great Hampstead parties full of celebrities, at which he could talk loudly in a booming voice about himself and how women threw themselves at him. Despite his youthful anarchism and bombast, he was touchingly delighted to be elected an A.R.A., albeit rather late. Like many psychological casualties of the First World War, he concealed deep traumatic scars behind a frivolous social exterior of enormous charm which responded eagerly to any sort of adulation. His friend Orpen, whose work was also affected by trench horrors, was not dissimilar; it was at a Nevinson party that a Russian girl, seeing Orpen's frantic public jollity, asked with the perception of her race why it was that he was so unhappy. Orpen was already drinking himself to death.

The heightened outrage with which Nevinson painted in 1915 was never repeated. His autobiography makes a brave tale of his post-1918 life, describing trips to New York, much mingling with the mighty, events in artistic society, the progress of Socialism and many illnesses, which were a legacy of his unhappy boarding-school youth. His book is very readable. His only child died, virtually in childbirth. Tonks continued to persecute; the art establishment did not ease its attitude. Nevinson was no longer a rebel, a progressive; his Cubist realism gave way to figurative art of little passion. He made money out of portraits. He was touchy but kind. He put on an exhibition of flower paintings which delighted his wife. His interests were wide and intelligent.

It is as though one were reading about an active pensioner, a retired man who started his retirement at thirty but believed he was still at work.

Failure is always relative. A man who could paint *La Mitrailleuse*, *The Road from Arras to Bapaume*, *La Patrie* and other war paintings, some from aeroplanes, quite apart from excellent Cubist skyscrapers of New York and things like *Henley Regatta*, hardly deserves to be called a failure. War heroes are not called failures, even though their lives may meander quietly after the medals have been awarded.

Artists, however, are supposed to go on developing; they aren't allowed to rest on their laurels. Critics are unrelenting in their scrutiny of creativity.

'It's not fair,' Sue said again, once I'd got home and calmed her down. I didn't go into too much gory detail and, somehow, things which happen abroad are not as immediate as violence here, in the street outside. Sue has reluctantly accepted my tendency to become involved in things which go violent. 'The art market doesn't think anything of Nevinson now. War paintings aren't wanted. His other stuff isn't powerful enough. There are lots of lesser painters from the 'twenties and 'thirties whose work is doing much better. He believed that society was against him and it seems as though he was right, even now.'

I tried to mollify her. 'It's no good getting upset, Sue. Art is always about fashion. I think the real problem is that the Nevinsons which come up at auction nowadays are all the lesser works, the careless or incidental stuff, so the market thinks he's not very good. The war paintings are all pretty well sewn up in the Imperial War Museum, the Tate and other galleries, or the Cadbury collection. You just can't get them. What's available is thin by comparison. I've checked through the catalogues of the last few years and most of the Nevinsons which have appeared at auction have been pretty duff.'

This was true. Jeremy had burst into my office to find me thumbing through a stack of art catalogues from the major auctioneers, compiling a mental collection of fairly dim images and an annotation of lacklustre prices.

'Tim! What are you looking for in those? The Ashworths have been asking what on earth's going on. You haven't forgotten them, have you?'

I put down the catalogue I was holding and looked at him wearily and meaningfully. 'Philip, you mean. Philip Ashworth. I expect he's been phoning you, has he?'

Jeremy blinked. 'Yes. How did you know?'

'Just an inkling I had. I've arranged to go up and brief him and his Uncle Jack together.'

Jeremy goggled at me for a bit before speaking, a bit quietly for him.

'Tim, there's been the most horrendous set of events. People strangled and slaughtered and God knows what. Yet here you are, cool as a cucumber—no, cold as ice—rootin' about in Christerby's catalogues. Uncle Richard's as harassed as I've ever known him to be about you. He says you've explained most things but he's sure you're keeping a lot back. Are you all right? You seem so, well, detached. I mean, everything's all right, isn't it? All cut and dried, from what Richard says of the Belgian and French police?'

This was also true. Traces of Kolewski and his reeking yellow cigarettes had been found in Janssens' car. Traces of Elizabeth van Laeten had been found in both Kolewski's and Janssens' cars. The staff at the Janssens factory had eventually and reluctantly provided evidence that Martens' work was being fed into their computers. Kolewski's bank account had unexplained credits which were being traced back to a Janssens source. A search of Bob Janssens' house, bank deposit box and private safe had turned up, piece by

piece, disks and programs and photocopies of Martens'
work. Malfait was jubilant and had sent further messages
of gratitude and appreciation. Elizabeth van Laeten had
gone, after questioning, into purdah. It was not clear
whether she would be charged as an accessory to industrial
theft; she had an alibi for the night Janssens was strangled,
when she was said to have been with a friend, so that did
not provide another possibility of judicial action against
her. My guess was that if Claessens had anything to do
with it, she'd not be charged. The French and Belgians
were trying to piece together Kolewski and Janssens' movements on that last, fateful night. Why Oudenaarde? Where
had Kolewski been?

There was still plenty to occupy my mind but I wasn't
coming out with it yet.

'It's all right, Jeremy. I'm not concussed, or in shock, or
anything. Just tying up some loose ends.'

He stared at me suspiciously. 'Loose ends?' He gestured
at the pile of catalogues. 'To do with painting, with the Art
Fund, perhaps?'

'Something like that. Funny how the Art Fund always
intrudes. We'll make a useful acquisition soon. But don't
worry: I'm not going to burst out in fireworks or something.
Not unless I'm forced to.'

That didn't please him, either. The suspicious look deepened. He opened his mouth, closed it, opened it again and
then thought better.

'Doubtless,' he said, with heavy dignity, 'in the fullness
of time you will advise me of any developments?'

'Kipling,' I said enigmatically, 'advises well on these circumstances.'

'Kipling?'

I put my head back to quote.

'If you can wait, and not be tired by waiting,
Or being lied about, don't deal in lies,
Or being hated, not give way to hating,
And yet don't look too good—'

'*Nor talk too wise.*' He finished it for me. His face puckered. 'You're certainly not doing that. I'll wait for when you're ready.'

'Thanks.'

My meeting with the Ashworths was for the following day, but at a more civilized hour than my first one. Over the top of Turton Moor the conifers seemed to bristle closer to the road as though to crowd me, and my inclination was to look out of the rental car upwards to my right, away from the dark spiky trees to where the bare hills' light green and patched colours were segmented by the ragged walls that kept sheep from straying too far. Darwen's chimneys pointed downwards to my place of arrival once again, clustered and remote, reminding me of how in days before salted, gritted and metalled roads, these towns had been so self-contained, close, inhabited by people crowded like families cheek by jowl together.

'You're dead on time,' Jack Ashworth said heartily, grasping my hand to shake it and wave at Philip, who came forward with his shy smile to shake carefully as well. 'Doris has got kettle on't boil ready for you. She said you're a punctual man, you are.' He grinned at me. 'I think you've made a hit with our Doris. So we'll have a cup of tea first thing.'

'Thanks.'

He cocked his big battered head to angle at me. 'You look well, considering. It's been a shocking affair, hasn't it?'

'It certainly has.'

Doris came in with the heavy tray, smiled at me, and bustled about, serving. A homely feeling pervaded the office. I took a swig from a thick pottery cup and eyed Nevinson's marchers on the wall. Soon I knew that they would be gone from there, down to the Art Fund's collection, and I stared to feel the keen anticipation that an acquisition always brings.

'Shocking,' Jack Ashworth repeated, his eyes on my face, more as a prompt for the inside information he was seeking than as a statement of anything he felt.

'Yes.' I got up as Doris left, thanking her, and went over to the Nevinson to look more closely at it. Lines and movement and tackle: he'd got them all, perfectly.

Jack Ashworth looked at me curiously. 'Still keen on that, are you?'

'Yes.' I turned back to him. 'Have I still got first option?'

'Of course you have.'

'Can I exercise it?'

He blinked at me. 'You mean you want to buy it, now?'

'Yes, I do. I'll give you a fair price.'

'Thank God for that.' Philip Ashworth's voice was slightly hoarse. 'Thank heavens. Get it out of the place, Uncle Jack. Take whatever he offers. Quick, before he changes his mind.'

Jack Ashworth eyed his nephew incredulously. 'What's up, Phil? Got the willies or summat?'

'It's unlucky. I want it out.' Philip Ashworth was tense. 'Quick, before he changes his mind.'

'Fifteen thousand,' I said, standing in front of it. 'The last good Nevinson was bought in at nine thousand, but he has gone up to thirty-six thousand for a good one. That's the best price ever. The market's down and he's not popular. I think fifteen thousand would be fair.'

'Done.' Philip Ashworth snapped the word out. 'Done. It's yours. Take it with you.'

'Here.' Jack Ashworth spoke softly, but he got his bulk quickly to his feet to face me. 'What's all this? What's all this about?'

'It's unlucky.' Philip Ashworth had gone blotchy, white and red spots burning on his face. 'You know it is. That's why it was put away for so long.'

'What's that got to do with the price of cotton?' Jack Ashworth's northern accent came back into prominence. 'There's been bugger-all bad luck to us since I hung t'bugger up. Others, maybe. But not us.'

His expression challenged his nephew. Philip Ashworth looked at him, dropped his eyes, raised them to look at me, then bit his lip.

'I think,' I said gently to Jack Ashworth, 'that Philip is referring to the death of your nephew. Two days after you hung that painting up.'

'Nephew?' Jack Ashworth scowled. 'What nephew? No nephew of mine's died.'

'I'm afraid he has. Pierre Martens. At Wingles, the day we met.'

I said it blandly, in a matter-of-fact voice, to try and keep the drama quotient down for him. I liked Jack Ashworth, cunning old trout that he may have been, and it wasn't fair to spring it on him in these circumstances, not really.

His face registered shock at first, then truculence.

'What the hell are you on about?'

'Your nephew. Philip's half-brother. He was called Pierre Martens. The strange thing is that everyone said how similar they were and I paid no attention. I thought it was because they were both computer freaks. But I've checked. Martens came from Roeselare, originally. He was illegitimate, brought up by a couple in Ghent. His mother was in the Resistance. Your brother Ted's Lancaster came down in Belgium. He survived for nearly two months behind the lines but then they were betrayed. Actually, the crew were taken to a textile factory where it was thought they'd be safe. But the Germans got them and killed them. Lancaster crews were not popular with the Germans. Martens' mother only heard what happened later. I don't think she really knew, or wanted to investigate too closely, who Ted was. To her he was just another fleeing airman she rather liked, but she didn't want to embarrass the family in England. She didn't know he might be well off. He was dead long before she had the child, registered it at Roeselare, and gave it out to be adopted. It was 1945 by then. Everything in ruins, or confused; people trying to start their lives again. But Pierre Martens, adult, very much later, searched and searched to find his background. He never married; something to do with being an orphan, I think; it affected him in the opposite way it does others. He was introspective and mathematical anyway. He located his mother after she'd died. He visited her grave quite regularly. I imagine he found out that his father was an RAF airman who was killed.' I looked across at Philip Ashworth. 'Then he met you.'

Jack Ashworth sat down heavily. 'I'm not taking this in,' he said.

'Your brother was fond of the poetry of Robert Graves. You said he always carried a slim volume with him. Even when flying. I think it was an old copy of *Fairies and Fusiliers*, published in 1917 when his grandfather died.' I was looking at Philip Ashworth, still. 'It was in Janssens' bureau bookcase. The initials E.A. were in it. I thought it was Edwin Ashworth's, from the First World War, but of course I was wrong. It was Ted's. Edward, not Edwin. The textile factory they were betrayed in belonged to Louis Janssens. Bob's father.'

Philip Ashworth said nothing. The spots on his face were fading a little.

'It's missing,' I said.

Jack Ashworth looked up. 'What's missing?'

'The book of poetry. Your brother's. Janssens must have taken it out. Or someone else did.'

Jack Ashworth shook his head. 'I don't understand this. Book of poetry? What does it matter?'

'Forty-seven years,' I said to Philip. 'You must be a year or so older than him.'

'Yes.'

'When did you find out?'

He smiled a little. 'When we had dinner together. At least, we guessed. Pierre had done a lot of research. Last year he found the names of the air crew who were shot—the RAF have marvellous records on things like that—but he didn't know which one was his father. Then we just had to look at each other.'

'Did he know about the Janssens factory? The betrayal, I mean?'

'He more or less guessed that, too. It was a place in Courtrai. Janssens were in an old factory then. One of dozens of them. There was a lot of confusion; collaborators were forgiven eventually, but not always.' He stared at me speculatively. 'My mother told me that my father always carried a copy of that book. We have others of Graves's books at home, all of them my father's originally, but that one's missing.'

'Where is it now?'

He frowned at me. 'How should I know?'

My tea was going cold, so I went across to drink it. I didn't know what more to say. I was frightened of asking too much. Had Pierre Martens confronted Janssens with the knowledge of his father's betrayal as well as the theft of his work? And Philip Ashworth, reserved and restrained, a technical man; the knowledge might easily have unhinged him, temporarily. The letter that Martens posted on the morning of his death was almost certainly to his half-brother Philip, revealing everything he knew. Yet when I'd asked him at Preston he'd denied any such knowledge. A man like Philip Ashworth, one used to working in the abstract, to bottling things up, might easily blow a fuse. I remembered the way he'd looked at Janssens when we met him in Janssens' office. He knew; I was sure he knew that Pierre Martens' death had been engineered from Courtrai. What had he done about it?

He would have to have planned, to have thought about it carefully, as a technical man might.

And he said to me, when I visited the Preston mill, that he didn't want that painting to cause the death of 'yet another' of the family. He'd known about Martens all along.

I thought of Janssens, brown and fit, being overpowered by the pale Philip Ashworth. Surely that couldn't be? Yet his hands were still a yachtsman's hands: corded with sinews, set on muscular wrists. It wouldn't have been beyond him to twist a scarf to a man's extinction.

'You must never tell your mother.' Jack Ashworth, with alarm in his voice, now spoke directly to Philip. 'It'd destroy her faith. She's never remarried, not for lack of opportunity, but because she worshipped Ted. We all did. She mustn't know anything of this.'

'I know. Don't worry, I won't.' Philip looked sympathetically at his uncle. 'Poor Pierre Martens is dead, anyway.'

'I'm sure we can rely on you, Tim?'

'Of course.'

Jack Ashworth got up, walked across to the Nevinson, took it off the wall, and handed it to me. 'I accept your offer. I've no doubt it's fair. Take this with you, will you?

As far as you can. I can't believe this properly yet, I can't really take it in, but I know what Philip wants.'

I nodded. I had a theory, when explaining things to Sue, that that poetry book might now be in Southport with Philip's mother, but I discarded it. Philip had probably kept it himself, to avoid difficult explanations. Most likely he took it off Janssens in his car, near Oudenaarde, having instructed him to bring it with him. Janssens would have had to attend the rendezvous, even if only to check how much evidence the Englishman had got. Philip Ashworth was supposed to be in Aachen, researching the German opportunity, that night. Aachen to Liége, thirty minutes. Liége to Brussels, an hour. Brussels to Oudenaarde, maybe forty minutes. Say two and a half hours at most. Probably only two. He could simply have strolled out of the hotel and disappeared in his hire car, returning five or six hours later. Why should anyone follow him?

I felt instinctively that Kolewski had almost certainly been with Elizabeth van Laeten most of the night. Until he came home and I met him, anyway. I didn't see Kolewski killing the goose that was going to lay his golden eggs, not even if there were amatory complications. It was Malfait who was his obsession, his cause for treachery. I could imagine him killing Malfait, but Janssens? The man for whom he was setting everything up? It didn't feel right.

He'd had a go at killing me, though, and what he'd done to Martens didn't bear thinking about.

Why choose Oudenaarde? Why make Janssens head towards Brussels rather than Roubaix?

Elizabeth van Laeten said she had an alibi. Well, she would, wouldn't she? She wouldn't want to be an accessory to the murder Kolewski was assumed to have committed.

Claessens would want to believe her. Any friend's testimony would do.

I took out an Art Fund cheque-book and wrote out a cheque for fifteen thousand pounds, a sum well within my own discretionary spending. Nevinson might be unlucky for the Ashworths but I'm not superstitious. I'd never have bought half the Art Fund pieces if I were.

Jack Ashworth looked at the cheque and put it in his desk. He and his nephew had gone unusually silent.

I got up.

'I thought I'd rather see you in person,' I said. 'The big carpet deal is all off but I hope there'll be other opportunities. You'll carry on your discussions with Hartmann in Germany, I expect?'

Jack Ashworth nodded. There was no comment on their backstage manœuvrings that I wanted to make.

'And Malfait has got himself tied into a new French deal. It's not clear whether Martens' work will continue.'

Philip was watching me intently. He moistened his lips very slightly.

'The Belgian police, and the French, say everything is all explained. The murder of Janssens is attributed to Kolewski and he's dead. I'll have to go back to testify, but that's only a formality.'

'Oh, aye?'

'Yes. It's all sewn up.'

Jack Ashworth got up slowly and held out his hand. For a man who had involved himself in a Belgian venture he'd never intended to complete, playing a fox's hand, and had received rather more information than he'd bargained for, he was a model of composed behaviour.

'I'd normally ask you to stop,' he said. 'See you were properly fed and watered. It's been a bit of a shock, though. I need a bit of time to take it in. I hope you'll excuse us?'

'Of course.'

'Philip and I have a lot to talk about. But next time, perhaps, we'll make up for it?'

'Sure.'

I took his hand, then held mine out to Philip. He took it gingerly at first, then grasped quite firmly. His hand was strong and sinewy; I let go of it rather quickly.

'Go carefully, Tim.' He managed to meet my eye. 'Give my regards to Jeremy. Tell him I'll be in touch about further help with the Hartmann deal.'

'I will.'

Who would be more intense? A great shaggy violent bear of a man like François Kolewski who could take women or leave them, had never married, or an intense technologist with a dead half-brother and a betrayed father to avenge?

I took the Nevinson carefully by the frame and went out into the cold car park below the private hills which look down on Darwen. The marching men went on to the car's back seat, oblivious, caught forever tramping, whoever they were, for their moment of anonymous immortality.

Every time I looked at that painting I'd think of where it came from, and what it meant, and what explanations I would have to give to Sir Richard and Jeremy, and repeat to Sue, who'd sat open-mouthed as I told her what I thought, last night. There was no evidence, no reason to fracture the careful shell of what had been evaluated and filed in Belgium and France. Janssens was dead and deserved to be: likewise François Kolewski.

All very neat and tidy.

But like some other paintings I've acquired for the Fund, the pigmented surface people would see and react to would never have the same effect on me. I'd think about appearances and things beneath them, things hidden and unsolved and concealed, somewhere below the smooth surface of life that instinctively we all prefer not to disturb, especially when there's nothing to be gained by doing so. Sometimes it's best not to be too clever, just as Kipling says, and to be content with keeping your knowledge to yourself, sweeping the dusty things out of sight.

Under the carpet, you might say.